Daniel Sidney Warner

# Poems of Grace and Truth

Daniel Sidney Warner

**Poems of Grace and Truth**

ISBN/EAN: 9783337407445

Printed in Europe, USA, Canada, Australia, Japan

Cover: Foto ©Andreas Hilbeck / pixelio.de

More available books at **www.hansebooks.com**

Your Saved Bro.
D. S. Warner

# POEMS

## —: OF :—

# GRACE and TRUTH.

## ⋗BY⋖

## ⋗D. S. WARNER.⋖

**ILLUSTRATED.**

# P*R*E*F*A*C*E.

POETRY is a Divine emanation.   The more a pure mind drinks in its Spirits, the more it will soar up in heavenly contemplation, and increase in adoration.   To awaken love for pure poetry, is to give an upward lent to its future life.

God has blessed the human family with many noble religious poets; but their productions are necessarily mingled with the shades of religious error that overcast their days   And God desires His people, and their children blessed with poetical thought on the summit of present truth.

In putting forth this new book before the public, we seek not nor expect to elicit any literal conpliments.   We have written for the edification of the common people, and not for applause of the critic   The work has been executed in the midst of constant evangelistic and editorial cares and labors, and having been written in our absence from home and library, it will be found nearly destitute of historical embellishment. But to the ordinary reader it will be all the better appreciated. We shall be happy and satisfied, if the instrument of these simple verses be esteemed less than nothing, if they will create in the reader a more exalted conception of the grace of God, and kindle in his heart a more fervent love for His truth.

This is the humble Prayer of

THE AUTHOR.

# TRUTH.

"Mercy and truth are met together; righteousness and peace have kissed each other. Truth shall spring out of the earth; and righteousness shall look down from heaven."—Ps. 85:10,11.

"And judgment is turned away backward, and justice standeth afar off: for truth is fallen in the street, and equity cannot enter."—Isa. 59: 14.

"And their dead bodies shall lie in the street of the great city, which spiritually is called Sodom and Egypt, where also our Lord was crucified.

And after three days and a half the Spirit of life from God entered into them, and they stood upon their feet; and great fear fell upon them which saw them."—Rev. 11: 8, 12

# TRUTH.

WHAT is truth? inquired Pilate, sober,
  Immersed in deep perplexity,
Trembling while in judgment over
  The one his final judge must be.
He asked, but waited not the answer,
  For in His majesty there stood
The Truth Himself at his tribunal,
  The incarnate Truth of God.


Eternal Truth, thy boundless glory
  The holy angels cannot sin.
But rapt by thy Celestial beauty,
  We must this feeble tribute bring;
For all this heart hast thou enamored,
  This humble soul with love enshrined:
Our life is laid upon thy altar,
  All thine our body spirit mind.

Shine on with all thy constellation,
　　The precious attributes of God,
Love, mercy, justice, and compassion;
　　For second in thy magnitude
Thou only art to love's effulgence.
　　"I AM the Truth," and "God is love."
From both in one omnific fulness,
　　Proceed the streams of truth above.


High honored, and from Everlasting
　　Thou art, O Truth, a pillar strong.
Upholding Justice, faith and virtue.
　　Before the stars together sang
Our ill-doomed planet's new creation,
　　Thy hand didst hold, on Heaven's throne.
The balances that weighed all nations,
　　Upon all worlds that round thee shone.


Thou art the firm and deep foundation
　　Of hope, and universal good.
And on thy broad eternal bosom,
　　Is based the awful throne of God.
The myriad stars that gem the ocean
　　Of boundless space, at thy command,
Pursue their even tenored motion,
　　And all supported by thy hand.

The clod we feeble insects cover,
  Once deep submerged in angry flood,
Now hangs in short disguised probation
  Upon the Truth, "the Word of God."
The secret's locked in Father's bosom,
  And marked in Heaven's calendar;
But present truth gives faithful larum
  That time has reached its evening star.

When first this jot of God's dominion
  Was sadly plunged in hell's control,
Truth dropped betimes some gentle beaming
  Upon the ruin of "Mansoul,"
Beneath a dark prophetic mantle
  He painted hope to mortal eyes,
And on His Blood be-sprinkled altars,
  His coming glory symbolized.

When long expectant, earth had waited,
  And all the nations musing sat,
In Heaven's secret council chamber
  Truth, love, and pity fondly met.
They kissed, as on her lonely orbit
  Earth moved heavy up the skies;
And, groaning neath sin's dark oppression,
  Held long their sympathetic eyes.

Then Pity broke the silence weeping,
    Love, deeply moved, to justice spake,
And mercy joined her interceding
    That fallen man for pity's sake,
Should now be ransomed back to Heaven.
    Then Truth rose up in majesty,
Thus saying, "I for man will suffer,
    Here Love and Mercy offer me.


"Great Spirit, give to me a body,
    A proper sacrifice for sin,
And thou, O justice! sum man's debit,
    And let me surety be for him."
Then answered Pity, Love, and Mercy,
    "O speed thee Truth, but not alone,
For we thy sisters will go with thee,
    And rear on earth thy peaceful throne.


The angels sang the joyful tidings
    To shepherds of the lonely night,
"Peace," highest boon to earth is given
    And wisdom came to see the sight.
The Truth has made his lowly advent
    Where falsehood sin and error held
For ages past destructive regent.
    "Good will to man" the chorus swelled.

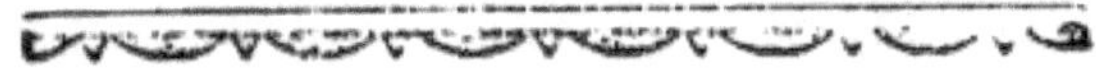

So Truth went forth with love and mercy,
  And freedom followed in their wake.
The chains of death and hell were broken,
  And tyrant thrones were made to shake
They built on earth a crystal palace
  Adorned with precious gifts Divine.
The Truth Himself its ground and pillar,
  Whence all His grace and glory shine

Upon the Mountain of His temple
  Truth sits the Judge of every creed,
And prime instructor of all people
  Who wish to gain true wealth indeed.
Thence all the wise and prudent hearted
  From earth and sea's remotest bound,
Go up to drink of wisdom's fountain,
  Whose streams with life and peace abound.

Here grace reveals the happy secret
  Of living pure and free from sin.
And gratitude to God upwelling,
  Her everlasting anthems sing.
Here ransomed souls obtain the glory
  That Truth enjoyed in worlds of light,
And hath bequeathed to all that love Him,
  E'er back to Heav'n He winged His flight.

When once enshrined within the bosom
  And deeply rooted in the heart.
All earth and hell can ne'er dethrone thee
  For thou, O Truth! so precious art.
What millions for thy sake have suffered,
  Yea, suffered to the martyr's crown.
But thou art worthy, Prince of Heaven!
  That millions more thy sceptre own.


In sack-cloth clothed, amid thick darkness
  For twelve hundred and three score years,
Thou didst bear witness with thy fellow,
  When pity seemed to have no tears.
Blood stained the earth along thy pathway:
  The throbbing life of holy hearts
Flowed out to seal thy spotless virtue
  Till hell, blood-sickened, thence departs.


But devils only quit the carnage
  To brew another policy.
Twas this, in feigned deceptive homage
  They bow to Christianity.
They aid by means, and willing counsel;
  But only lend a helping hand
In hell's own int'rest, Truth to Martyr,
  And the Church of God to strand.

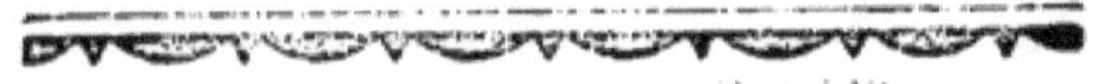

The pit-devised abomination
  Erected in the holy place—
More foul than gory inquisition—
  Confounded Truth with sin's disgrace,
And mixing up in vile confusion
  The works of God and devils too,
Gave birth to o'er six hundred factions,
  A God-profaning babel show.

Pure Truth declined in this malaria,
  The Spirit, ling'ring, deeply swooned,
Till both were stabbed in sect-Gomorrah
  And fell, alas! with mortal wound.
So hell "conceived and uttered falsehood,"
  While "Justice standing far off weeps"
"And judgment is turned away backward,"
  "For Truth is fallen in the streets."

Their bodies lay in Sodom, Egypt—
  Lay prostrate in her streets in state,—
For just three hundred years and fifty,
  Which time we've seen expire of late.
While lying dead, o'er them exultant,
  The town was filled with festive mirth
Because these prophets sore tormented
  All them that dwell upon the earth.

But Truth crushed down shall not forever
　　Lay martyred, trampled on the ground,
Though she bleeding falls,and seems extermined,
　　Eternal years are yet her round.
From each reverse she must relumine:
　　When buried she "springs out the earth."
For "righteousness looks down from Heaven,"
　　And glory crowns her going forth.


So the Spirit of life from Heaven
　　Entered, and Truth stood on His feet.
And with Him rose His fellow witness.
　　Then falsehood howled; for sure defeat
And woe befell her sinful nations,
　　Who love to make the Truth a lie,
And strive to think hell-born traditions
　　The very truth of God on high.


Then Truth put on his holy armour,
　　Unsheathed his mighty flaming sword
In war on every creed of error,
　　On full six hundred mixed and stored
With hoary lies and new inventions,
　　Where every Word of God's belied.
Each some truths contain, versing others,
　　So all is owned and all denied.

In some were taught that the Almighty
   Had fixed from all Eternity
Just who is lost and who elected,
   By His unchangable decree.
That some were born for dark perdition
   And others born for Heaven's plain,
And irrespective of volition,
   Each must that destination gain


That all the deeds of this probation,
   If black as hell or very good,
Are no prelude to future station.
   Naught but the pre-decree of God.
That He likewise had made selection
   'Mong them that die in infancy,
A cherub this should be in glory,
   And that inhabit misery.


This God and man-bemeaning doctrine
   Truth smote to earth and stamped upon.
And burst its hell invented fetter.
   So that even in old babylon
Its horrid face is deeply covered
   Neath moldy antiquated creeds.
And sinking deeper in oblivion.
   As worn out dogmas truth succeeds.

Long 'twas held that sects were holy,
  Their origine believed Divine,
Revered as gods, all rights of conscience
  Were laid devoutly on her shrine.
Her priests were clothed in superstition,
  And worshiped more than God on high
And he who bowed not them subjection
  Must for his high presumption die.


When evil stalked within her border,
  "Hush! hush! do not the Church deride
For by her sacred holy order,
  All her sins are sanctified:
Her jealous schisms and contentions,
  Her many rival altars round,
A healthful zeal imparting friction,
  Make grace and righteousness abound."


'Twas deemed an orthodox confession
  That grace and sin go hand in hand,
Throughout the years of our probation,
  Until we reach the better land.
That none may hope to gain a freedom
  Until our last expiring breath.
But sin in thought and word and action
  Till saved in the instant of our death.

These old opinions, rags and rubbish,
  All thread-bare, filthy, false and vain,
Were but a nasty heap of fuel
  For the Divine consuming flame.
And so He burned them all together,
  And left instead, as in her youth,
The Church that Jesus built forever.
  The pillar and the ground of Truth.


Instead of party name and faction,
  And rival clamor "here," and "there."
God's Truth brought fort his great salvation,
  And all the ransomed, pure and fair,
By love's Celestial bond, united
  In sweet and pure harmonious praise.
Truth reigning in each happy bosom,
  Behold they're one in all their ways,


He smote all sinnership religion
  And blasted every groundless hope.
Demanded present full savation,
  Or else abandon every prop.
He drew a line of demarkation
  Twixt every soul of sinful spot.
And he accepting God's election,
  The righteous man that sinneth not.

His hammer smote the black partitions
  Until they crumbled into dust
His fire made a conflagration
  Of every idol made their trust.
He then restored in all its beauty
  The palace He had reared before.
All cleansed and garnished, pure and holy
  And filled with glory evermore.


All must receive, who here would enter
  A circumcision in their hearts.
Repent, and leave all creeds of error,
  Have truth illume their inner parts.
Lay down their lives on God's pure altar
  And make the perfect Sacrifice
Of earth, and self, and sin forever
  *And buy the truth at martyr's price.*

# TWO SCENES AT THE ALLEGHENY.

---

ALONG a winding path there came,
A band of saints in Jesus name,
Leading downward t'ward the flowing river;
The rock-paved Allegheny stream,
Whose oil-blotched waters flow between
Tow'ring hills that drop upon her mirror.

Adorned in His own holiness,
Who first "fulfilled all righteousness,"
True discip'es of the Great Examplar,
Came here to show their love to Him,
By burial in the crystal stream:
Resurrected in His life forever.

The trees that emulative rose,
From bank to summit's high repose,
Waving in the sunlight's golden glory,
Displayed to their enraptured eyes
A thousand tints of richest dyes,
Varied in sweet Autumn's gorgeous beauty.


A hymn flowed o'er the water, still,
And echoed on from hill to hill;
Rising upward to the throne of Heaven.
This was the song that sweetly breathed,
Their praise to Him their hearts believed.
Even Christ, with whom their souls had risen.


Down into the flowing river,
Lo! the Lamb of God we see.
There He speaks in clear example,
Take the cross and follow me.


Cho.—Gently buried with my Savior,
Let me sink beneath the wave.
Crucified to earth forever,
Hence alone to God I live.

Now the sacred waters cover,
  O'er the holy Son of God.
Thus He washed me in the fountain
  Of His sin-atoning blood.

Crucified with my Redeemer,
  Now I sink into the grave.
I am dead to sin forever,
  By the life of God I live.

Here I witness a confession,
  As I merge from human s'ght,
In the tomb of yielding water,
  That the blood has washed me white.

O how sweet to follow Jesus,
  In this ordinance to show,
That we're cleansed in life's pure river,
  Even whiter than the snow.

To Him who said that every where,
  He wills that men should offer prayer,
By this emblem of the tomb of Jesus,
  His humble saints then meekly bowed,
  Amid the awe decorumed crowd.
Richly favored by His loving presence

Then one by one were downward led,
  And numbered with the sainted dead,
Pilgrims happy in the Lord's approval.
  Anew the Spirit of their God,
  Bore witness to the cleansing blood,
Making lofty hills with praises vocal.

  But some who stood beside that stream,
  Recalled to mind another scene.
Thirty years had fled along unceasing,
  As flows the water o'er that spot,
  Where red intemp'rance left a blot.
Time and tide have passed, yet unceasing.

  A husband, father, genial friend,
  But demonized by liquor fiend.
Deeply by this maddening viper bitten,
  Unto his home, near by this shore,
  Returned, rum-fired as oft before:
Driving thence his own in terror stricken,

  Three daughters fled adown the ledge,
  And spied the skiff at waters edge.
Boarding this they rowed into the river.
  To utmost strength they plied the oar,
  And hastened to the farther shore;
Praying God from wrath and waves deliver.

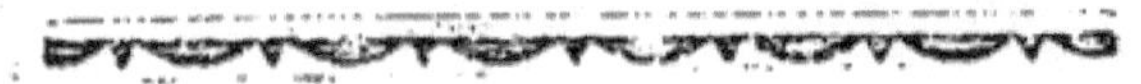

The frenzied came with angry mein,
To drown his children in the stream.
Breathing threatening, stagg'ring mid the billows,
The mad-man heedless onward surged
Till in the depth at last submerged:
Drowning there, a warning to His fellows.

Behold the contrast 'twixt the scenes!
The first in mem'ry sadly gleams,
Over thirty years that flowed unceasing;
As flows the water o'er that spot.
Where dread intemp'rance left a blot,
Time and tide have passed yet unerasing.

Baptized in spirits from the still,
Led captive by the devil's will,
Into awful death he plunged a victim.
From thence raised up a lifeless clay
His Spirit fled in wild dismay;
Leaving in that stream a doleful requiem.

But these immersed in Heaven's light,
In garments pure and spotless white,
Follow joyful down into the river,
The steps of Him who died on earth,
To give their souls a Heav'nly birth;
Burial deep in Jesus' love forever.

He, dead in sin and lost in woe,
They, dead to sin and white as snow,
Both were buried in this river's bosom.
His name dishonored floats along,
They rise to sing redemption's song.
Praising Him who gave their spirits freedom.

He builded there a monument,
Of liquor's black and fiendish bent;
Casting on that tide a gloomy shadow.
They leave upon that sacred shore,
Foot-prints of Him who went before,
And His blessing leaves a brilliant halo.

Behold two ways divide our race,
The road of sin, and path of grace.
Choosing this, or that to thee is given.
Both these ways dip in death's cold tide,
And judgment sits on yonder side,
Bending that to hell, and this to Heaven.

# THROWING INK AT THE DEVIL.

"Then I turned, and lifted up mine eyes, and looked, and behold a flying roll. And he said unto me, What seest thou? And I answered, I see a flying roll; the length thereof is twenty cubits, and the breadth thereof ten cubits. Then said he unto me, this is the curse that goeth forth over the face of the whole earth: for every one that stealeth shall be cut off as on this side according to it; and every one that sweareth shall be cut off as on that side according to it. I will bring it forth, saith the Lord of hosts, and it shall enter into the house of the thief, and into the house of him that sweareth falsely by my name: and it shall remain in the midst of his house, and shall consume it with the timber thereof and the stones thereof."—Zech. 5: 1-4

# THROWING INK AT THE DEVIL.

A T Wartburg Castle sat a Son of Thunder
   Dealing Heaven's Dynamite.
When lo! before him 'peared an apparition
   Fury threatening Demon sight.

The piercing words of truth, so long be-
   Flashed the burning wrath upon [smothered
The devils patent monk and pope religion,
   Who confronts the dread reform.

A thousand years of stupid chains of darkness
   Bound the devil in his pit.
His creeds and bulls held fast the world in bondage
   Leaving him at leisure.

That thousand years, thought yet to come in ba-  [bel—
  Fancy pictured reign of peace—
Passed while the souls of martyrs, 'neath the al-  [tar
  Waited till the evening grace.


While earth groped on in darkest superstition,
  Ruled by cassock, cowl, and priest,
Few souls had life for satan's bent to slaughter,
  Chained him from wanted feast.


But with the early gleams of reformation,
  He in person re-appears
His int'rest trusted not to deputation,
  Quickly breaks the thousand years.


Before the dauntless, lion-hearted Luther
  Forth the hellish monster stood,
Drawn from his prison by the scattering thesis
  'Gainst the Romish viper brood.


He lifted up his eyebrows knit with thunder,
  To the hellish spectre said
With stern address, "DU BIST DEN WAHRE TEUFEL."
  Hurls an inkstand at his head.

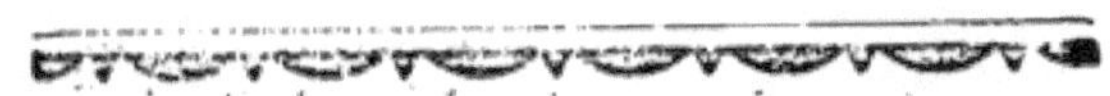

How potent proved the Doctor's splatt'ring missile,
  Hist'ry leaves us no memoir.
But ink he threw on paper at the devil,
  Battered down his kingdom more.


Still on in mercy moved the Great Eternal,
  Re-instating Heaven's truth;
Long fallen in the filthy streets of babel,
  Trampled under foot, forsooth.


A season passed of mingled light and darkness,
  Counted neither day nor night.
With each reform break in more gleams of bright-
  Loosing satan more to fight.      [ness.


But now at last the fogs and mists are scattered,
  And the sanctuary purged.
The hidings of the devil thus demolished,
  By the hail he's sorely scourged.


The dragon forced to open field of battle,
  Driven from his final trench.
Can't throw up another line of babel,
  Thence from storm of truth to flinch.

He would, 'tis true whitewash his sect divisions
   Pass them for the holy bride.
But truth uncaps the wicked corporations,
   And her founder cannot hide.


The light reveals her blood in every quarter,
   And she's strewn with dead mens bones;
Remains of souls that long have fed her slaughter;
   Hell with many a victim groans.


Thus chafed to anger like a beast of fury,
   When denied a skulking den,
And tantalized by thunderbolts of fire,
   Satan writhed within his pen.


At last he breaks the chains of self possession,
   Doth his best what time he hath.
Well knowing that he's but a little season,
   Comes he forth in utmost wrath.


Now loosed his imps o'er all this earth are swarm-
   But retreating toward the brink,       [ing;
Driven back by truth in thunder rolling,
   And the rapid flying ink.

Not as did the sturdy Whittenburger
    Fling his inkstand at the foe,
But by the mighty force of steam, much faster
    We the battle ink can throw.


At a point where two lightning tracks lay crossing,
    Northward, southward, east. and west,
God has planted there a Campbell mortar
    Firing ink at satan's crest.


This enginery by modern skill constructed,
    Hath a strong capacious fount,
Whence ink, by rollers to and fro conducted,
    Into ammunition count.


The ink rolls o'er ten thousand silent voices,
    All in rank and file complete;
When touched, each one prepares His trump for
    But refraining, tells the sheet.        [sounding,


The sheets borne round by cylindric motion,
    Take the type's impressive kiss,
Inspiring them with love and truth's great mission,
    And salvation's perfect bliss.

Not only toward the main fourwinds of Heaven,
   Sin consuming ink is shot;
But right and left in force, 'tis outward given,
   Striking sin in every spot.


When round, "Mansoul" Emanuel plants His
   To retake the famous town,      [army,
On "eye-gate" hill He plants this mighty engine,
   Till surrendered to His crown.


If chance a pilgrim's shield of faith is drooping,
   And his heart with fear oppressed;
Then comes the ink-winged angel, trumpet sound-
   And his soul anew is blest.      [ing

# MEDITATIONS ON THE PRAIRIE.

In the summer of 1872, the author took a mission field in Nebraska, much of which had just been settled the previous year. Our companion had died one year previous. Just before going west a correspondence was arranged with sister Sarah A. Keller, which soon kindled into a glowing flame of love A year later I returned, and we were happily joined in marriage. With her precious company came again to this blooming plain, where one year was sweetened with the most transporting conjugal bliss. In 1874 we returned to Ohio, where life and labors flowed on in uninterrupted happiness, until in 1884, the dear object of our love was deceived by the wily foe, and torn from our soul: a crisis that threatened our frail life, and which we only survived by the grace of God.

In the fall of 1887, while on an extensive western tour, we came into a new part of the great prairie, which strikingly reminded us of our travels on the new plains fourteen and fifteen years before. There the Spirit touched our mind with vivid recollections of that cherished one, who made for us this prairie a blissful Eden. An inspired imagination also portrayed what dire wreck of our own life might have ensued from the crisis of broken love, had not the grace of God averted the sad issue. This cast us on the sod beneath a load of gratitude, where the poem was inspired, as our heart's humble tribute for Heaven's pity, and sustaining Arm.

"Blessed be the Lord my strength, my goodness, and my fortress; my high tower, and my Deliverer; my shield, and He in whom I trust." Amen!

The Stockwell referred to in the poem, was a young preacher we doth had loved, who became puffed and deceived, and was the chief instrument of satan in the overthrow of companion's soul. As soon as we renounced him he dropped all profession.

# MEDITATIONS ON THE PRAIRIE.

GOD! what miriad thoughts arise within
My breast, and fool my soul to utmost brim.
Nor here confined, within my bosom pent,
The streams of thought and feeling forth
    are sent:
    As when a fountain pressed by ocean head,
    Or subterranean stream, by mountain
    torrents fed,
Updwelling in tremendous force, and flowing
A river, by a thousand tributaries growing.
Our feeble speech, a tube diminutive,
Through which a mind some thoughts to mind may
    give,
Can only bear a streamlet from the flood,
That issues from a soul inspired of God,
Ah! could the soul a scope of language find,
That would convey to fellow human mind,

The boundless volume that it issued forth,
Swelled by streams that head in heaven and earth!
But mind, a part or faculty of soul,
Cannot transmit the fulness of the whole.
So language, formed by finite intellect,
Is vastly for the soul inadequate.
Our words but signalize imperfectly
The blessed visions that our spirits see.
As signs of ideas, tell but meager parts,
Of what we inward feel, to fellow hearts.

Thank God for One to whom the human breast
May pour out all, and sink to hallowed rest.
Each want, though inexpressible and deep,
He reads and fills with love and grace replete.
And all our conscious debts of gratitude
That lade our heart, made pure in Jesus' blood,
Though greater than our lips can e'er express,
Our souls may bring to Him in righteousness.

Man, formed to hold converse with God on high,
Who reads the mystic meaning of a sigh,
And all the scroll our deepest feelings write—
A volume ever hid from human sight—
May pour to Him the torrents of his soul,
Of which man takes a part, but God the whole.
For God and man possess a language, deep,
Unwrit on earth, nor man with man can speak.

So here my soul upon this prairie vast,
Roams far abroad, then up to Heav'n is cast.
Like some swift boat with precious lading speeds,
And brings from distant port its country's needs,
So mounts, with freight of gratitude to Heaven
My heart, and then returns with bounties given.
Our thoughts soar up in meditation's flight,
As meekly bows the Sun to introduce the night.
O praise the Lord for all His mercies felt and seen!
For this virgin plain so modest, fresh and clean.

The jungle deep, and scrubby thicket maze,
Seem formed for knaves, who shun the open gaze.
As late encountered in Missouri's wilds,
And dark monotic barren oaken hills;
No hundred miles from that notorious place,
Where murd'rous banditi made their name's a curse,
The lawless mob, dark masked, and hell inspired,
Came on our quiet midnight camp retired.
Led by satan who retaliation sought,
For the loss his kingdom suffered on that spot.
Because expelled from many souls he'd found,
Ordered us to leave the consecrated ground.
Such scrub oak haunts seem fit environments of hell.
While on this plain but holy saints should dwell.
Here all is naked, open to the eye,
The green carpet intercepts the fleecy sky.

Save by night, all must walk in neighbor's sight,
While thickets cover darkness day and night.
Where actions lay exposed to human gaze,
It puts restraint against pernicious ways.
All men should know that darkness covers not
Their deeds from God, who sees the hidden plot.
And that our steps are viewed by human eyes afar
Should remind of Him who seeth every where.
Yet even on this fair and verdant plain,
Men curse their souls with blackest foulest stains.
In rascal schemes the west all earth excel,
The multitude are racing on to hell.
Vile rogues here purchase lands of honest fools,
Agree to pay the price in well broke mules,
Then ship to their enraged and 'stonished view,
Cast-iron stock, with each a broken limb or two.
No fable this, nor isolated case
Of hellish frauds and wills that keep apace
With the driving rushing occidental speed,
For pelf and every base and sensual greed.
So e'en this pure delightful prairie scene, [mean,
That should rebuke each thought and act that's
The fiend hath used to fill the heart with lust,
In taste gloat for canker eating rust.
While oft within the rustic woodland cot,
The hand of Providence is ne'er forgot.

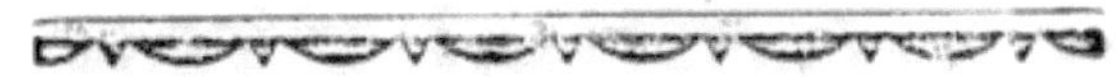

There walled about by barren rocky hills,
Man, blessed with poverty's contentment, tills
And reaps his little range of fertile nooks,
That nestle in the streamlet's fork and crooks.
No avaricious thought o'erleap the bounds
Of those hills, that fix the limit of his grounds.
In honest sweat he eats his daily food,
And pays to God his debt of gratitude.

   Behold that scene ye wretched prairie sharks,
Whose craving well nigh 'grudge the meadow larks.
A place to light and sing your Makers praise,
Gods yourselves ye'd rather be o'er all you gaze.
Is this the tribute you return to God,
For the blessing of this verdant sod?
Fix ye no limit to your selfishness?
But crave, and rob, and cheat and dispossess
Thy fellow men far as thine eyes can see,
Of homes God gave to them and not to thee.
And He that gave hath noted thy defrauding rooks,
And thy extortions, in His judgment books,
Which soon will open in His final court:
There summoned, all shall give a strict account.
That day will search thy heart's most secret springs,
In perfect balance weigh thy blackest sins.
The poor oppressed shall at that bar appeal,
And find redress from thy oppressive heel.

Ye wicked, who by stealth your coffers fill,
Will there be sentenced to eternal hell.
    O think ye dwellers on this beauteous land,
How much ye owe your Makers loving hand.
Turn now thy mind toward the rising Sun,
The rugged woodland coast, where first begun
Thy sires, with hearts of iron hardihood,
To charge upon a thousand miles of wood.
They swung their steel in cheerful honest toil,
And let the sun-shine on our freedom soil.
In vain the red-man's knife, and warlike dance,
Nor forest trees withstood their bold advance.
They faced the lofty phalanx's fearful odds,
Commanded by the ancient oaken gods.
Though angry storms they'd braved from tiny birth,
They bowed their crest and shook their mother earth.
There lay their pondrous trunks with many a limb,
On charged the woodland ants to chop and trim,
To log, and pile, and burn the trash away.
Your fathers sweat and labored night and day,
Mid reeking fires that drew the painful tears,
Each cleared his farm by patient moil of years.
Its not the easier thing a man can do,
Existing in a woodland country, new.
"Nature—who moved in first, a good long while—
Has things already somewhat her own style,

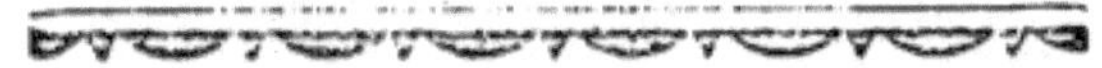

And she don't want her woodland splendors bat-
Her rustic furniture broke up and scattered,[tered,
Her paintings, which long years ago were done
By that old splendid artist-King, the Sun,
Torn down and dragged in civilization's gutter,
Or sold to purchase settlers' bread and butter.
She don't want things exposed, from porch to clos-
And so she kind o' nags the man who does it. [et—
She carries in her pockets bags of seeds,
As general agent of the thriftiest weeds;
She sends her blackbirds in the early morn,
To superintend his fields of planted corn;
She sails mosquitoes—leeches perched on wings—
To poison him with blood-devouring stings;
She loves her ague-muscle to display,
And shake him up—say every other day.
She spurns his offered hand with silent gibes,
And compromises with the Indian tribes;
(For they who've wrestled with his bloody arts
Say Nature always takes an Indian's part.)
In short, her toil is every day increased,
To scare him out, and hustle him back East;
Till fin'lly, it appears to her some day,
That he has made arrangements for to stay;
Then she turns 'round, as sweet as any thing,
And takes her new-made friend into the ring,

And changes from a snarl into a purr:
From mother-in-law to mother, as it were."—*
    There sat the woodsman on his cabin sill,
When dusky eve had bid his ax be still,
And cast his eyes toward that timbered spot,
Where all the day his utmost strength had wrought
There, on that tow'ring front of living green,
Scarcely a perceptive change is seen.
Then gazing round upon the small domain,
Which he'd released from sturdy timber's claim—
And that contested yet by roots and stumps—
The poor man's courage falls into the dumps;
His bosom sighs, until at last it breaks
In words, and thus, addressing wife, he speaks.
    "I've just been thinking Jane while sitting here,
How we shall live until this land is clear.
How long and hard we both have worked, and now
We've not a spot where roots admit the plow.
I took my ax this morning feeling strong and well,
And thought I'd make this day of clearing tell,
But looking over there it seems to me,
After all I've done I hardly miss a tree.
I fear that we shall both be in our graves,
Ere where that timber stands, the wheat will wave.
Things look mighty woolley, and our prospects blue,
Can you tell me how we'll weather it through?

*CLINTON.

"Well John, 'tis true we cant see far abroad,
Yet from our nick we can look up to God.
And this we'll do, we'll trust Him by His grace
Beyond this rugged woods He hides a smiling face:
The very trees so thick, and tantalizing high,
That mock our hope and all our strength defy,
Were planted by our Heav'nly Father's will,
As sentinels to guard against a greater ill."

"True, wife, we should no providence arraign,
But think how nice, were this an open plain,
There's no sale for wool, and I can't understand,
Why 'tis piled up here so thick upon the land,
We chop and n'gger, grub, and wear our lives away,
And often lift until we see the stars by day.
When once we sow upon our fallow clod,
Our bodies too are ready for the sod."

"Nay my husband do not thus repine,
Or sit in Judgment on the Lord's design.
Hope, our strongest shield against despair,
Needs some wise restraint, lest soaring in the air,
And building many lofty castles there,
Reaction comes, she falls and proves a snare.
Subverted hope, transcending reason's altitude,
Like the Lit., dips, flounders, plunges in the mud.
So were this land all free from nature's growth—
Which to encounter men are even loth,—

What bounds would then thy sanguine raptures find?
Extravagance would paint her picture in thy mind,
Of highly colored vanity and lure,
With caution, prudence, and economy obscure.
And thinking riches treasured in thy lap,
Thy healthful toil to indolence would slack.
Next on thy place dread mortgages would rest,
Far worse encumbrance than the timber pest.
   "Worms or beetle—drought or tempest—on a
         farmers land may fall:
But for first-class ruination, trust a mortgage
         'gainst them all."—*
   Then count no more these trees of value naught,
They stand a faithful guard around thy cot,
And check those flighty sanguine nymphs of hell,
Which o'er the prairies roam about at will;
Inflating men with fancied thriftiness,
And robbing them of what they do possess.
 Excited hope runs headlong into delt,
Then slides its victim in the bankrupt pit.
You vainly wish this woods were all an open plain,
But foresee not what evils there might reign.
Would not snakes hiss and rattle by the million,
Because no sticks and clubs at hand to kill them?
So John you see there're drawbacks every where,

                 *CARLETON.

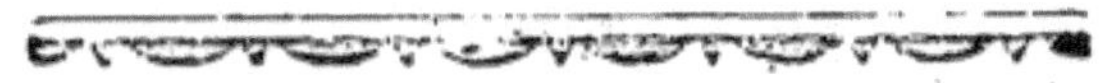

But contentment is the best to keep the weather fair.
Stockaded round by nature's rough environments,
We owe yet much to nature's Providence."
    Thus spake the weary yeoman's noble wife,
And raised his drooping spirits into life.
Such were the scenes oft witnessed, when of yore,
Settlers felt the wolf's dread gnawing at the door.
Still to their task they bared their brawny arms,
In years of toil, e'er plenty stored their barns.
Out of forest wilds, by muscle strong as steel,
They hewed a nation, free from tyrant's heel.
    Thus a thousand miles of wood were cleared away,
And sunlight entered from the closing day.
Astonished, cried the woodsman, "Lo! I see
An open world with neither shrub or tree.,"
What can this be?  A desert vast and drear,
A barren, empty, worthless, hemisphere;
An ocean wide of parched and naked ground,
With scarce a spear of vegetation found;
Save on the margin of each crystal stream,
A long and winding thread of living green.
    But shall this vast expanse be ever waste?
And yield no blessing to the human race?
Nay, God reserved this broad and lifeless plain,
Till no spot remained for yeomanry to claim.
Then He who "turns a fruitful land to barrenness,"

Because of man's presumptive wickedness,
Now touched the silent desert by His hand,
And lo! it blossomed as the rose at His command.
First appeared the little downy "buffalo,"
Following on the meadow grass began to grow.
Then the all creative smile of God
Sowed His variegated flower seed abroad.
And a thousand miles of floral garden poured
Their fragrant incense to Creation's Lord.
Whose artistic skill imparts every hue
Of purple, crimson, violet and blue.
Whose exquisite pencil streaked the flowerets,
And touched with uniformity their sets.
Rare plants of lavish care in eastern room,
In this waving sea of beauty grow and bloom
In their wild profusion, only tended by
God's hand, and his own beauty loving eye.
Here all the cactus family abound,
Their monstrous leaves spread out upon the ground.
Beset with needles, like the devil's tongue,
And with alluring floral goblets hung.
The mountain shadows fall upon the cactus shrub,
A loosely woven perforated wood.
    The rosin lifted high his golden crest,
A floral world its gracious Maker blest.
Then came the lark, and all the feathered throng,

And, inspired, broke the silence with a song.
Men looked again. Behold! how changed the scene!
Long slumb'ring nature sudden springs to green.
God made a new edition to our world,
Good tidings to the homeless thus unfurled.
And as a starving herd rush through the fence,
When opened to a pasture rich, immense,
A million "prairie schooners" presto steer
Toward the flower-land, from brushy tangled clear.
And all ye trains with awful blazing eye,
Drop down your track, as vivid lightnings fly,
And pour your streams of emigration, brought
From all the world, and as by magic dot
This vast domain with its unnumbered homes.
Here new-born hamlets swift to cities rise,
To all past human progress a surprise.
Thus, after lumb'ring on in feeble might,
"The star of empire westward *takes her flight.*"
    Hear now ye restless prairie demi-gods
Who ne'er have blacked your hands on "niggered" logs,
Why foul your souls, upon this Eden land,
All pure and fragrant, ready made to hand,
Grass-set and leveled to the shuttle knife?
The loving flowers blush at your ingratitude,
And shocking sin against Omnific Good.
    Though no rugged bows hang threatning o'er thy head,

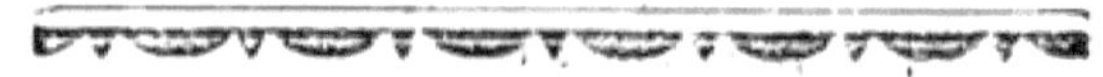

Fing terror's shaft will lay thee with the dead.
The tarantula, hairy devil shape,
With dreadful poison menaces thy fate.
And lurks the still more deadly centiped.
To-day, who knowest, his bite may end thy greed.
The bracing winds that paint thy cheek with bloom,
May chant thy solemn requiem to the tomb.
Repent thy folly then, and Heaven's wisdom share,
So thy heart shall blóssom like this prairie fair,
And He who wisely checks with drouth thy wrongs
Will bless and cheer the land with harvest songs.


But what the muse has given us to sing,
Is scarce begun, and shall we now begin?
O must this feeble mind attempt to draw
A scene so deep of bliss, of woe and solemn awe,
With only straitened words at our command?
A scene unearthly language would demand?


One year had passed since death dissolved the bond
That firmly knit two souls in love so fond.
Still bled the sundered tendrils of our heart,
It seemed a trying providence to part.
Pure and modest as the summer's setting sun,
Our sweet walk of five bright years seemed just begun.
But He whose wondrous grace and love can heal

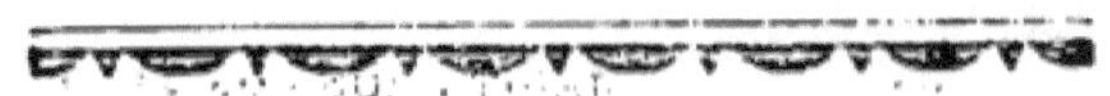

Our wounds, and all infirmities can feel,
And ruleth all in Heaven, and earth, and hell
By His own wisdom, and benignant will,
And thus vouchsafes to His peculiar seed,
That all must work for good to them indeed,
Now touched the fountain of that heart bereaved,
And wrought a mystic change that quite relieved.

   How strange that Tanzon—name in mem'ry blest
Should hold no more within affection's breast
The place of wife. Yet love, on higher plain,
With angels bright associates her name.
Amid the scenes of Heaven's paradise,
We hold thee not by these terrestrial ties.
And thus reveals the Spirit of the Lord,
How it can be as written in His Word,
That when the tenuous thread of life's dissolved,
Surviving one is from that law absolved.
Next unthought whispers dropped from Heav'n's
     throne,
We should not complete our pilgrimage alone.

   'Twas at this time the Spirit's voice revealed,
This new-homed plain should be our mission field.
And to the call we westward bent our way.
But just before, upon a Sabbath day—
A thousand times that favored day we blest;
For from it sprang love's plant within our breast.

A fountain head it proved to us, unknown,
From which a crystal stream of bliss hath flown—
In company we walked the pasture sod,
To meet in worship 'at the house of God.
O'er head the sunshine smiled peculiar sweet,
And nature's carpet soft beneath our feet.
Our course lay winding 'long a pleasant glade,
And birds were sweetly singing in the shade.
There chanced—or Providence had so designed—
To drop an only one with us a pace behind,
A sister, modest, pure, of guileless piety,
Of deeply marked religious family.
And though her face rare charms of beauty wore,
Her graceful form but plain apparrel bore.
We talked of our prospective mission, far,
The storms and dangers we might hazzard there.
And just before we reached the sacred place,
Came this beautiful thought 'twould be a mear so
If blessed with a christian correspondence  [grace,
With one of such sweet tempered innocence.
What of int'rest in our travels to relate,
We deemed that hand so kind would compensate.
The boon was asked, an I gained the fair's consent,
Undreamed as yet our Fathers wise intent.
Then taking leave of friends and brethren all,
I set forth toward the field of duty's call,

Tho' her face rare charms of beauty wore.
Her graceful form but plain apparel bore

Aboard the chariots of prophetic fame,
All "running like the lightning" in their train.
As predicted is this preparation time,
How they wou'd fly, with "flaming torches" shine;
And so swift their meted time would make,
That by their course, most terribly would shake
The fir tree: agitated by the riven air,
Rushing wild to fill the vacuum in the rear.
And looking out upon the landscape round,
Trees, fences, buildings, even mother ground
Seem frightened, panic-struck, and taking flight.
Hills like lambs, skipping, fleeing out of sight,
All creation like a sweeping avalanche,
Breaks loose in front, and pellmell rearward rush,
Whirled back as by the fury of a hurricane,
While beneath two rails as lightning stream.
Thus borne along, as by the wings of time,
We mused upon the deep prophetic chime
Of holy seers, who in this message all agree,
Just e'er time's transit reached eternity;
On lightning trains swift flying angels would
Mid heaven sound aloud the trump of God.
Thus gathering into one the true elect
From every fold of babel creed and sect.
  On we sped toward the day's expiring gleam,
Transflying father-river's mighty stream,

Hurling broad rich Iowa into the rear,
Behold! Nebraska's virgin plains appear.
When crost the western tributary, dark,
We quaffed the air upon this fragrant park.
Here gazing round, far o'er the valley Blue,
Our optic nerves soon painful weary grew;
Because no distant object intercepting rose,
Kindly bidding vision stop and take repose.
Lo! here immortal souls we usual found
In two successive earthly temples homed.
The outer turf-brick or sub-earth "doga,"
The inner their terrestial mortal body.

To promise true those welcome letters came,
    Here then we published Heaven's holy Word,
Inviting wayward men to come to God.
And not in vain;   for many a ransomed soul
Was written down in Heaven's living scroll.

    To promise true those welcome letters came,
And cheered the traveler o'er the lonely plain.
Each one that winged its journey to and fro,
Seemed with deeper words to burn and glow,
'Till both were forced to own, from friendship's seed,
There'd sprang the Eden plant of love indeed.
Still growing up and spreading rapidly
Sweet blossoms, folded up in modesty
Adorned this holy tree of paradise;
These blooming into love's ecstatic bliss.

The case was plain, nor could the secret rest,
Silent, smothered in the enamored breast.
Love hath a voice, and hath a list'ning ear,
Knoweth when to speak, knoweth love will hear.
Love, pure, Platonic, Heavenly, Divine!
What ecstatic raptures in thy temple shine!

"Almighty love' whose nameless power,
    This glowing heart defines too well,
Whose presence cheers each fleeting hour,
    Whose silken bonds our souls compel,
Diffusing such a sainted spell,

"As gilds our being with the light,
    Of transport and of rapturous bliss;
And almost seeming to unite
    The joys of other worlds with this,
The Heavenly smile, the rosy kiss;—

"Before whose blaze my spirits shrink
    My senses all are wrapped in thee
Thy force I own to much, to think
    (So full, so great thine ecstasy)
That thou are less than deity." *

*Tennyson.

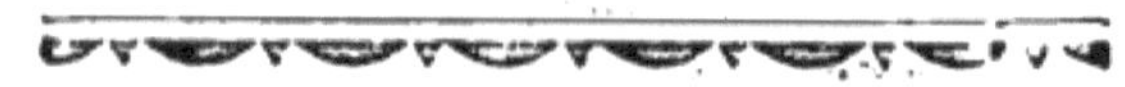

Beyond imagination's bright forecast,
This love thirsty soul was satiately blest.
All o'er this bright inspiring floral plain,
Where e'er our circling pilgrimage had lain,
At morn, at noon, in evening's sacred calm,
In village street, or driving o'er the lawn,
By day or night, alone, or in the multitude,
Before our eyes that form of beauty stood.
The mournful cooing of the gentle dove—
Meek, honored symbol of high Heaven's love—
Baptized our Spirit in an ocean tide,
Of love, that winged its object to our side.
The singing lark, so cheerful, sweet and clear,
Oft 'lighting, by its welcome notes to cheer
Our way far o'er the prairie, blank and raw,
Seemed the voice of her my vision saw.
Without thy smile, thou fair and lovely one!
O what were I?   a world without a sun.

    Did Tennyson "of fair women dream"—
Lo! our eyes of the fairest one have seen—
"Of those *far*-renowned brides of ancient song"
Oft dreamed we of one as fair, a *present* one.
Present?   yea tho' a thousand miles away,
Her angel spirit lingered found my way.

    'Twas fixed in Heav'n and here on earth well  known
Two happy spirits into one had flown.

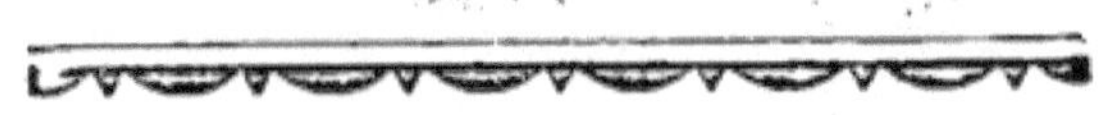

Two souls united by love's golden band,
Now offer to each their heart and their hand.
But one reservation we did record,
"To thee I give all, but highest my Lord,
As Savior and God, my heart must enshrine;
In the path of His will, my dear I am thine."
"All thine, and forever," the fair replied,
"My life and my fortune to thee I confide."
A thousand "God bless dear Sarahs" were breathed,
Ten thousand God-thanks for the favor received.

The months slowly past, oft counted ahead,
When eastward again our journey would speed,
And time wing us back to the dear beloved,
Whose rival tried heart so constant had proved.
Like Jacob when serving for Rachel his charm,
We waited our year, abiding the time.
While weekly we quaffed the pure nect'rous cup,
(Their sweetness me thinks e'en angels would sip,)
That flowed from a hand that was warmly moved
By love's holy flame, and devoutly loved.

Time wore away, and the last Sabbath came,
That held us in duty upon this plain,
The sweet Gospel labors it brought were done,
And our heart ached sweetly as sank the sun.
His bright glowing face seemed smiling with cheer,
To welcome the close of our exile year.

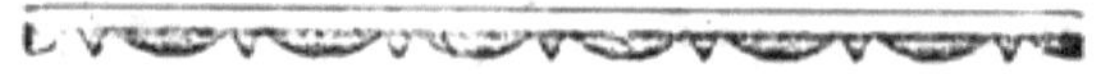

We watched his sweet sparkles like gold in the mint,
Till twinkling in the grass his good night squint.
We slept 'till orient gleamings bid us rise,
And fly away to our adored prize.
  O let my soul, and all within give praise,
For the hand that marketh our sun-lit ways!
Next to the gift of Heaven's only Son,
I glorify Him for this sweet pure one,
In whom such charms and virtue all combine,
That it seems presumption to call her mine.
Transfixed we gaze upon those eyes and ween,
"Is this a dream of some unearthly scene?
Nay, 'tis real though marv'lous in our eyes.
Hath God bestowed on us this great surprise?
  The blessed hour came, and side by side we stand,
In solemn grateful joy each grasped the hand
We prized above all others 'neath the sun,
To men confessed that God had made us one:
For long e'er this, in Heaven's court was sealed
Our union, only now on earth revealed.
  Thank God for one trace left of Paradise!
Found in the bliss of a devoted wife.
As sung by one of Heaven's favored bards
When tuned by his Delia's fond regards.

  "What is there in this vale of life,
  Half so delightful as a wife,

When friendship, love and peace combine,
To stamp the marriage-bond Divine?
The stream of pure and genuine love,
Derives its current from above;
And earth a second Eden shows,
Where e'er the healing water flows."—*

"The Wife! O, could I but rehearse
Her praises in immortal verse,
Who, trusting in man's plighted truth,
Will leave the loved abode of youth,
Will leave a mother's gentle care,
Life's good or ill with him to share;
For him leave all home's tender ties,
Its pleasures and its sympathies!
Yes, all, though tears her eyes bedim,
She leaves, to brave the world with him.
If down life's stream he gently glide,
She's ever joyous by his side:
Her cheering smile and gladsome voice
Tell how she can with him rejoice,
And thus make life's short journey seem
Bright as wild fancy's brightest dream.
But oh! if adverse storms arise,
And storms o'ercloud life's brightest skies,—

*COWPER.

When all which once seemed bright and fair
Brings disappointment and despair,
When friends are false, and foes are strong,
To heap upon him shame and wrong,—
When all unite in filling up
With bitterness life's mingled cup,—
She bears with cheerfulness a part
Of every grief that wrings his heart,
And e'en when humbled to the dust
Cheers him with words of hope and trust.
Like Gertrude, she will by him kneel
When gasping on the bloody wheel,
And from him will not severed be,
When in his deepest agony.
But as the tendrils of the vine
Around the oak more firmly twine
When the keen blast most fiercely blows,
And rages 'mid the leafless boughs,
So does the wife still closer cling
To man amid his suffering;
And when he yields his dying breath,
She has a solace e'en in death. "—*

Flesh of flesh, and bone of bone, O mystery,
If not Eden, tell me what thy name may be.

*William Baxter

Deeper, higher still thy sacred chords entwine,
Merging twain in one, spirit, soul and mind.
O love-angel, native of high Heaven's throne,
Thou hast a mathematic system of thy own.
Not one and one make two, as school additions run,
But by thy rule, O love! one and one make one.
And should vile demons from the pit presume
To rent this warp and woof from Heaven's loom,
The sequel, "one from one leaves naught" 's untrue,
Alas! by love's subtraction, one from one leaves two.
  The round of blissful nuptial visits paid,
And all our friends and brethren farewell bade,
Two happy mortals in new life begun,
Wheeled our chariot toward the setting sun,
And here upon this free and sun-lit plain,
Love found her realm of pure Edenic reign.
With her most happy reinforcement blest,
We resumed our mission labors west.
A million flowers smiled along our way,
The feathered songsters, more than ever gay,
Commensurative of our happiness,
Tuned all their gleeful melodies afresh.
The silver luminary of the night,
Seemed as the noon-day sun in glory bright.
While the king of day in heightened splender shone,
In combined force of seven suns in one.

The stars that sang the joyful celebration
Of this terrestrial planets new creation,
More than e'er embellished the nocturnal skies,
With all their myriad twinkling eyes.
Thus the majestic heavens day and night,
Dropped tributes to the feast of love's delight.
And all mundane objects wore a floral bloom,
To heighten and congratulate our honey moon.
    Nor did that moon e'er wan or hide her face,
As months and years sped on their rapid pace.
For time's strong hand makes all but true love old,
Its wealth more indestructible than gold.
When in fire molten takes more lovely mold,
And endures till the heart itself is cold.
Each passing week but added fervency
To its pure flame.   And our felicity
Wrought in us deeper, warmer gratitude
To the Benignant Giver of such good,
On us, so undeservedly conferred;
So o'er the plain our songs of joy were heard.
The year we traveled on this blooming plain,
Embalmed it in our mind as love's domain.
Love added beauty to the meadow green,
And colored bright the gorgeous evening scene.
The sunset spread her bright vermilion dyes,
In awful grandeur on the western skies.

And fleecy clouds sublimely rose in white,
With golden tinge, to heighten love's delight.
She sparkled in the dewdrops of the morn,
Gilded universal nature with her charm.
Her magic seemed to sport with nature's law,
And on the landscape scenes of beauty draw.
The summer miraged groves of shady green,
While tranquil rivers winded round between.
And often on our 'raptured vision brake
The lovely mirror of a crystal lake.
With goodly trees upon its curbing ground,
Reflected on its silver bosom round.
These illusions to the eye so perfect placed,
That thirsty pilgrims o'er this lonely waste,
Turned their weary feet toward the prospect fair,
To slake their thirst beneath the foliage there.
But th' receding picture, mocking their approach,
Soon vanished, when, behold! again encroached
The empty plain instead upon their stare,
When hope, thus baffled, turned to sad despair.
  King-winter spread his crystal glory too.
Each distant object lifted high in view.
The morning sunshine on the glitt'ring frost,
Its wondrous scenes of silvered beauty cast.
Bright pyramids, and steeples in the sky,
And obelisks, magnificently high.

These crystal beauties images appeared
Of that bright fervent love our hearts endeared.


At last the providential time had come,
To leave our rustic little prairie home :
And eastward flying o'er the broad domain,
We welcomed old familiar scenes again.


Full thirteen years has gone to ages past,
Since wife and I beheld this sunny west.
There came an epoch in our christian state,
News that we were willed a boundless rich estate.
We blessed the tidings of surprising gain,
Our title proving clear put in our claim.
'Twas granted, duly sealed in Heaven above,
And proved the heritage of perfect love.
O wondrous grace that we should now possess
The Kingdom and the glory of perfected holiness!
Who could augur that heaven would bestow
Such sweet fruition on His saints below ?
All inward foes expired, and swept away,
All darkness fled, and left eternal day.
In this holy walk with Jesus, peace is giv'n,
Exceeding all our brightest dreams of Heav'n.
This greater, purer, sweeter grace Divine.
Still warmer did our hearts in love enshrine;

For grace ne'er destroys but quickens, sanctifies,
Brings 'neath the Spirit's rule, the natural ties.
Then persecution waked from slumbers deep
Poured out its vile aspersions at our feet,
Along the high and holy path we trod,
In hope to turn us from the light of God.
These only sank us deeper into rest,
And undisturbed repose on Jesus' breast.
Each taunt we suffered for our Christ Divine,
Made brighter still His glory in us shine.
Our bark was launched in a heavenly stream
That daily varied in delightful scene.
Some years thus past in the beautiful tide
Of love and bliss that more than satisfied.
Elected thus by grace and providence,
Hope flattered us with coming blessedness.
But ah! vain man, this wisdom timely learn,
Lean not on earth whose tide adverse may turn,
And sudden change the aspect of thy life,
From prospects fair to sorrows deep and rife.
    Lo it came! a stunning billow unforecast,
An awful storm, a fell satanic blast.
Hell in counsel struck his dark infernal plan,
Neath preachers garb concealed the woeful ban.
First there appeared, mysteriously withal,
Some leprous spots on our domestic wall.

The plague soon marred our holy fellowship,
Then ate like moth the threads of love that knit
Our hearts and souls in sweet connubial bliss,
And made us one in sympathetic flesh.
O infernal spirit! 'guised in subtile light,
How camest through the line of Heav'n's vigils
Into our pure domestic paradise,              [bright,
Now spreading here thy bane, and fell devise,
Despoiling rudely our embrosial bower,
Our wanted joy o'er casting with thy lower?

   O sweet departed angel—*harmony* !
May we again thy sacred hov'ring see?
O gracious Father! search my bleeding heart,
If ought thou findest caused thee to depart,
Lord sweep it hence, what e'er the sacrifice ;
Give harmony, well bought at any price.
Why now doth she, true helpmate hitherto,
A course so mystic, and so changed pursue?
O why this picking, carp, incessantly,
And concealing what the fault may be?
Why the dear one's sad and dismal moan,
Alternating with novice Stockwell's groan?
O my Father! must we hear it day and night?
Hints and whisperings telling, "he's not right,"
Slanting looks that dark suspicions cast,
Yet keep the devil they imagine under mask?

Either she we dearly love, we can't deny,
Must be deceived—O can I think it!---Or 'tis **I.**
Sad conclusion, a worse could ne'er betide,
A dilemma dark as hell on either side.
Were we to choose which one of twain it were,
Prove me the lost, O God! but honor her.
Dare I suspect that one beloved so dearly,
One who so late was in the light so clearly,
That her discerning was to me for eyes—
That gift in her we'd marked with great surprise—
Dare I presume that she I did esteem
The chief of holy saints, an angel queen,
Could have possibly been lately overthrown,
And brought this dread confusion in our home?
    O gracious Providence! what e'er of woe,
Whatever dark and cruel storms may blow,
Or hellish monster rush upon the keel—
With mad intent to blast and sink the weal—
Of our domestic bark that sailed beneath
Love's banner, fair, and her celestial peace,
Most of all we deprecate, and implore
Deliverance from the verdict daily forced the **more,**
That she we held immaculate in soul,
Is led captive 'nea'h, deception's dark control.
    Nay, I must cast the painful thought away,
And rather judge myself, unknown, astray.

Then, desperate grown, here Lord we humbly kneel,
And pray, O God! our family plague reveal.
If still my heart thou seest unsanctified,
Reveal the worst, then let the blood applied,
Purge from our home the dark accursed thing,
That harmony and love their wanted fruit may bring.
O that ' *If* " (unused in seven years of grace,
And covenanted ne'er to give a place,
Yet now allowed for sake of her we loved,)
A breech became, a dreadful darkness proved.
Four and twenty hours we felt the dread converse
Of faith's tranquility, we'll not rehearse.
  The shield recovered, lo! the Nazarene
Spake, "Peace, be still! " all sank to sweet serene.
But still there lurked around our household plague,
Nor hushed the dropping accusations, vague.
Moaning, groaning, dubious talk aside,
Satan gathered into darkness, then denied
That I were saved at all, but sore deceived,
Which, her unwilling to suspect, I believed.
Bewildered thus in old Despair's domain,
We feared that hope would never smile again.
Before the Church we humbly prostrate fell,
There beseeching God to break the horrid spell.
That moment, lo! in joyful sweet surprise!
Jesus blest, and bid us trusting thence arise.

N r did this yet suffice to make us own—
Swift self to judge . but others to improne—
That we vainly sought to assimilate,
With spirits that counseled to precipitate
Our soul into the net of hellish power,
Our strength to crush, our peace and hope devour.
Oft as by shield of faith, and Spirit's Sword,
Some footing gained, we in turn, its loss deplored.
At last God spake, "Wouldst thou successful run,
Then Christ thy Head, thy wisdom must become."
True Lord!   This lacking we've suffered hitherto.
Thy wisdom give! O God the boon bestow!
Then answered Heav'n in solemn awful tone,
"Wilt thou my wisdom take? lean on it alone?"
A moment's dread hung trembling on our mind.
What's there so awful with this gift combined,
That its tender should be clothed in such appall?
Our quaking soul shrank tempted to recall
The gift implored, lest it forsooth include
Some whitened furnace flame not understood.

    But O thou great and dreadful God,
    Are not thy mercies deep and broad?
    Then like thy ancient singer, we
    To thee from men and devils flee.
    Though awful round about thee Lord,
    Thy favor can alone afford,

A refuge for my hunted soul.
O God I bow to thy control,
Thy wisdom give what e'er the cost,
Or, O dear Lord! my hope is lost!

The Heavens bowed and sweet assurance gave
That, after tried, such wisdom we should have,
In which, henceforth our tranquil soul immured,
Should be from masked infernals well secured.
The dreaded climax came, the testing woe,
'Twas when assembled, saints and devils too;
The fuddled prophet spake, by hell inspired,
And blinded souls his fulsome lies admired.
The house was filled with 'wild'ring babel fogs,
For out the grumbling prophet's mouth, "like frogs"
Came evil witching spirits, more than three,
And wrought hallucination's trickery.
On the lounge a hid'ous horror lying,
A woman, frightful, blind, and nearly dying.
Her lifeless eyes were sunk, her phiz grimaced,
Deep moaning, as by serpents coil embraced.
Behold that Brother—late so good and true—
Depicting woe, as if to hell he'd broken through.
His limbs distort, as by rheumatics drawn,
His countenance bescowled, woebegone.
What means this strange phenomena? was asked.

The whimpling prophet, with eyes to Heav'n cast,
And with a grave and sanctimonious mein,
Prognosticated on the mystic scene.
"'Tis, said he, "God's mighty pow'r manifest:
Not in vain He's caused this marvel on us rest,
A wondrous work, no doubt on some one here,
He would perform, just who He'll make't appear.
Then each of tender conscience 'gan to say,
"Lord is it I? Lord is it I, or nay?"
Some were present needing much salvation,
Yet no subject for this great occasion.
Each in preferment wishing neighbor's call,
Gazed round to see on whom the choice would fall.
The Spirit regend there me whispered thus,
'Tis doubtless for thy sake this pow'r's on us.
If now with wisdom's gift thou wilt be blest,
Just let thy bosom's want be here confess'd"
'Twas accepted, unseen its foul intent,
We owned our soul's pursuit, and humbly bent
A suppliant in that infernal maze,
To evil spirit's much elated gaze.
The household head of anti ordinance
Delusion, darkness all his high pretense,
His dwelling was a congenial resort
For hobgoblin, spirits and every grade and sort
Of unclean birds and beasts.   And such the crowd.

Stockwell, exultant o'er us 'fore him bowed,
Standing in high priests' officiation
Critic'ly pried into our consecration.
This question, surmisingly propounded—
Then disgusting "a ha"s forth resounded—
'Do you consent to sell the Gospel Trumpet?"
"Yea Lord! sell, or by thy counsel give it."
"Nay but R. (one with demons dark possessed)
Greatly wants it, and is able to invest.
We feel that this is Father's firm decree
And perhaps He can't reveal 't unto thee;
Therefore be wise and act upon our light."
"I will.   Dispatch for R. you may this night.
One condition.   Should God, e'er the transfer,
Interdict thy order, His we will prefer."
Nay but that "if" reserve you must leave out,
Then God will greatly bless you we've no doubt."
In that hour hell displayed his subtlety,
Reasoning that submission were humility.
Quoting Scripture as to our Redeemer.
"Yea all of you be subject one unto another."
The chicanery of the devil fiercer raged,
Adroitly on our sympathy engaged,
By cunning craftiness our soul to crush.
"Yield, then these dreadful cries of pain will hush.
Submit thee to the will of God on high,

"Or if rebellious these may even die."
    A small mysterious circle intervened,
'Twixt us alone and all who there convened.
This will cast round in mercy to protect,
The foe turned on our conscience to suspect
That we were wrong and they were sons Divine,
No fellowship extended o'er the line.
She, thought next to Christ, a pillar to our soul,
Without our orb, joined in the blind condole.
Some saints, till now so dear, to our surprise,
Stood off and stared on us with evil eyes;
For their imaginations whirled around
By hell's caprice, on whom he willed they frowned.
The cunning stratagem availed once more,
Our stultified and blinded will gave o'er.
In that maze of devils who could cooly think,
'Till rushed along upon the very brink
Of denying God in us His Sovereign right.
We dropped the "If," and plunged our soul in night.
Then ceased the dying agonies.   The yeaing
Gave place to fiendish laugh, like mulish braying.
In vain they looked to see the promised blessing—
Infernal waves, instead, our soul depressing—
Disappointment brought reflection to its throne.
Conscience, reason, sense, Bible, all disown
The papal *Ipse dixit* came from God.

Hence instead of light came the chast'ning rod.
And who 'rt thou by dragon pow'r installed pope?
That thou presum'st with the Almighty cope
And durst forbid that His effulgent beam,
Should thy ignoble mandate contravene?

The assembly broke in satisfaction to
The mixed throng, and to demons, as they knew,
Or thought they knew, God's flying roll was taken
By the gates of hell;   no more to waken
Souls in false hope slumbring, and exposed to hell.
So demons in their frantic orgies yell.
But where was I?   Of strange bewilderment
Possessed, as if in hell's invironment.

We retired, not to rest, much less to sleep.
We sank beneath the billows, dark and deep,
Of an infernal sea, where dragons lay,
All mocking at our vain attempts to pray.
The varied horrors of that dismal night,
We've even wished were banished from our sight,
Blotted from that dark page of mem'ries book.
The terrors of that night o'er tophet shook.
O God let not the muse here linger long,
But pass this doleful tremor of our song!

A while we lay, hard gasping for our breath,
Darkly imprisoned, and half crushed beneath
The sleepers of an ancient crazy building,

Whose foundation, the structure scarce upholding,
Were decayed, ill-placed and toppling blocks,
And all seemed sinking to the earth and rocks.
Around us loathed corruption manifold,
Earth, timber, all o'er spread by nauseous mold,
Darkness, filth and suffocating humidness,
With danger imminent combined in wretchedness.
Seeing, through the small aperture neath the sill,
The counter passing tread of earthly drill;
And, in the sunshine of the world without,
Hearing gleeful chattering, and the merry shout,
All added aggravation to the gloom,
Made black the horrors of our living tomb.
No change of dismal scene brought in relief
To our soul, thrust to hell, alarmed with grief.
Now turned into lead, or petrifaction,
Of which our actual bulk were but a fraction,
Death menaced us beneath our ponderous weight.
'Twixt earth and hell we hung trembling at our fate.
    Here I pause that night's infernal record,
Our obsequiousness thus scourged of God.
    Nor were these flighty dreams of troubled sleep:
No slumber had that visit to the stygian deep.
Nor are they products of creative fancy,
The mystic treasures drawn upon by Dante,
And bards who fed upon imagination:

As if no poets' theme in God's creation.
Why plume the wings of thought to soar in vapor,
When subjects real more honor the Creator?
Why weave a thing of naught to grace a poet's diction
When facts are far more wonderful than fiction?
    In struggling prayer the seeming age was spent,
Yet conscious that to God no prayer upwent.
If thence been held to merge on faith's condition,
We should ne'er have seen mercy's fruition.
O His wondrous infinite gift of grace!
Unhoped, unexpected, ungrasped by us,
The morn suddenly flashed in streams of light,
And swept far away the horrors of night.
Praise "Him that maketh the seven stars of Orion,
Turneth the shadows of death to morning,
And that maketh the day dark with night,"
And speaketh the utmost darkness to light!
    The prophet's blind edict vanished as quick
As demons that brewed it fled to the pit.
    Now joyfully loosed from the sport of devils,
Our soul unprisoned. and free from trammels,
We leaped forth in the air with a shout of praise,
Hied to the office, and bowed grateful knees.
Lo! the heart and will of God then opened deep,
Forth down, down we sank. swallowed up complete.
As a child plucked from death, by love embraced,

Our soul, in the bosom of God encased,
Heard, "I'm now thy wisdom's impervious wall,
Gainst all devils transformed in light withal.
    Then understood, thank Heav'n! our soul full-well
Why that question on our mind with terror fell.
"Do'st thou truly take me for thy wisdom now ?"
This ordeal was needed e'er learning how
Our foibling trust in creatures to disconnect,
And reliance on God the Lord to perfect.
O sweet wisdom!  Thou God the fountain art!
Thy Son the stream now flowing in my heart!
    One day passed with our body, mind and soul,
Locked completely up in God's direct control.
Nor voice, nor tongue had pow'r to speak or sing,
Except as moved by Him who dwelt within.
Sweet silence, or words He chose to speak,
Were the hush of Heav'n, and freedom so complete.
But words were few throughout that holy day ;
No needless talk God loves, simply yea and nay.
    O what clouds of dread perplexity dissolved,
And painful anguish fled since we resolved
To dismiss all sponsors, and crouch no more
To demi-gods, our conscience ruling o'er.
A miracle Divine, in a manner loosed
The sacred tie that His hand had produced.
Pledged to our safety, Father could not see

An honest soul destroyed if to set 't free,
He must undo, if need be, His own seal,
When subverted to a poison in the meal,
And satan's chord to draw us to perdition;
Though dear 'tis sacrificed for our salvation.

But lest the tempter here should take occasion,
To throw, in trial's night, a dark suggestion
On hearts, where busy fiends their arts employ,
Wedlock's holy bond to sever and destroy,
We qualify these lines in righteousness,
And own the marriage law yet sacred over us;
Which but death, and one dark sin, can sever.
And then 'ts a serious question whether,
Even in the one condition stated,
One may be to a second living mated.

So then be it forever understood,
That we are still one lawful flesh and blood,
So long as both our heart pulsations throb,
And we revere the holy Book of God,
No tempting thought, or wish, or stray desire,
Shall to another's heart and hand aspire.
Nay, God forbid that we should ever aid,
Or lend a sanction to the cursed trade
In courts, where human flesh and Sodom bills,
Are bought and sold as lust and mammon wills.

Our ransomed spirit only then gave way

Its hold on one in error's path astray.
And ceased our fond but fruitless care to mend
A fellowship of spirits that can never blend.

Thus raised above all dark depressing pow'rs,
Sweet peace, and rest, and victory was ours.
But even now with broken fellowship,
We should yet, in nature's pure affection, sit
And love each other, neath one friendly roof;
For this but nature's ties should be enough.

Nor did the fierce engagement here yet close,
Infernal hosts in accusation rose;
Yea! hell seemed all her haunts to 'vacuate
And marshall black, this trusting soul to take.
"Woe to him who dare ignore and resist
"My servant, my great oracle and priest!
"It is presumption thou shouldst countervail
"My awful prophet, and not before him quail."
"Besides the Church and thy own flesh agree,
"That to him you should humbly bow the knee.
"Be warned and to his counsel now return,
"Or thy soul be lost, and thou a wretched kern,
"Shalt roam about in darkness to thy tomb,
"And sink at last to woe and endless doom."

Thus howled the dismal spirits round our soul,
Assuming Heaven's name to force control.
While these dread larums rang their doleful knell,

O'er our mind and soul were cast the shades of hell.
Wrought up conscience swayed wildly to and fro.
Then rememb'ring Him, our wisdom's glow,
"We'll die, O God! or thy good pleasure know."
We escaped, e'er the dawning from our chamber,
More urgent than from fire, the soul in danger.
In the office kneeling, besought the Lord
To end this question by His Spirit's Word.
Resolvent not to rise upon our feet
Till knee-bones, piercing flesh, the floor should greet,
If need be, e'er Almighty love and pow'r,
Brush back the mists of this satanic hour,
And say, by gracious voice from Heaven's throne,
If us the Trumpet's blast He'd choose and own.
O God Omnipotent!   Drive! O drive away
Those powers of hell that hold their dismal sway,
Like circling walls, than Babel's more immense
And o'er arched by ranks of diabolians dense!
To penetrate the arch of devil fog,
And see beyond the smiling face of God,
Whose eye  alone must guide in this affair,
Seemed a task fated but to sad despair.
Long wrestling hours had forced no cranny through;
Till grasped our hand the Book Divinely true,
And holding fast 'till faith identified
The volume with its Author, and applied

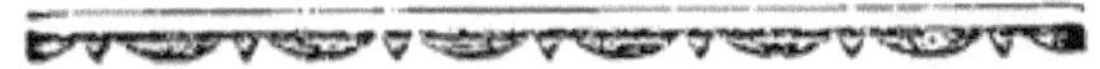

Some gracious promise to our pressing need,
And gave the silent ink the voice of God indeed.
That voice, more sweet and precious than the song
Of angels, heard by our rapt soul, ere long
Completely banished from our moral skies
The amassed force of devils in disguise.
And with them cleared the Stockwell mists away,
The pompous order fled at break of day.
But with return of night-shade's covering drew
Up the legions grim the battle to renew.
Yea! reinforced and more infernal grown,
Hell's fury rushed upon this soul alone,
Till one week's conflict wore our strength away,
And fears, like spectres, that we'd fall a prey,
Moved a prayer that Providence some friend engage—
It one left—to bear us from the battle's rage.
God heard, and sent that day one He'd reserved,
Who had not bowed to Baal, nor had he erred
In judgment rendered on that vaunting seer,
Nor had withheld the danger from our ear.
The forewarning the Lord through him had given,
Furnace flames had from our mem'ry driven;
Though the selfsame trial was the thing foretold.
On looking in his welcome face, behold!
His discredited larum fresh appears,
Bursting wide the seal of pent up tears.

He entered.　Speech failing, each to each was dumb.
This broke at last the silence;　"John it's come;"
No explanation necessary deemed.
The premonitioned storm at hand was seen.
This said again we silently conversed,
With floods of trickling tears that freely burst—
Thank God for tears! relieving as they preach—
From hearts too full for any other speech:
Mine with grief; 'stonishment and pity his,
Moved by our sad and sorrow stricken phiz.
Our grief rehersing silence thus went on
Till broke by, "Can I go home with you, John?"
"Yes," sobed out with more pity welling up,
For a brother drinking deep the Joban cup.

　　Seven miles away reached his domicile,
Ent'ring a hallowed Presence spake, "peace, be still!"
Soothed our driven spirit with a calm sweet
Converse of war and woe.　O rest complete!
There angels seemed come to minister and greet
Our war-wasted form, soon wrapped in sleep.
That hour, O how sweet!　First of good repose
Through that engagement with infernal foes.

　Let fancy now this picture thee portray,
A soldier's frightful week of war's dismay;
Robbed of sleep, hungry, under deadly fire,
Weary, wounded, death menaced, naught to inspire

A single hope that life can long endure.
From that hell of war him opened up a door
Where peace, rest, love and friendship smile around,
And safety ends the dread of battle ground.
  Ah!   this some faint comparison may hold,
To our happy transmutation yet untold.
O that blessed sweet and shelt'ring night!
When hell rolled back and Heaven rose in sight.
Sleep's only change, transporting dreams
Of boundless bliss and pure angelic scenes.
As if our soul had quit this vale of strife,
And entered to the joys of angel life.
Awakened by the thrills of holy love,
Our soul still lingered mid the scenes above.
  The conflict o'er, hell's counsel gates defeated,
The legions black then sullenly retreated.
Returning home, He reigning now within
Proved more than hell against our soul could bring,
'Neath our feet Almighty grace the dragon trod,
That serpent old, accuser, for our God.
The oil of gladness, a river flowing
From the throne of God, forever glowing
In bright sunbeams, where angelic anthems roll,
Filled with glory all the kingdom of our soul.
But the joy that made our heart with rapture swell.
As tormenting hail upon another fell.

The daily sacrifice, so richly blest,
Gave half my wedded being heart distress.
The more our soul o'erflowed in praise,
A face became more haggard with amaze
'Twas evident another crisis must ensue:
Either she must catch the holy fire too,
Or at least escape the plague that genders pain,
At sound of God-inspired praises to His name.
Or this alternative—and this alas!
Though least expected, came indeed to pass—
That one e'er held so dear must flee from home,
And seek relief within a cooler zone.
Having made on error's wing a lofty flight,
To a fancied and third-heavn's light,
Assumed our pedagogues, head, and eyes,
'Twere too painful from Capernaum's skies
To descend to one so like "a child that's weaned,"
Who'd on her judgment so unmanly leaned.
Unwilling she, to make the sacrifice,
For that fellowship we'd buy at any price—
Yea had thrice purchased, and yet unpossessed,
Its despoiler lurking in another's breast.
   The unhappy woman fled the sacred place
Of home, and our domestic throne of grace.
Weeks grew to months, with promise now and then,
"I'll come when that is past, or 'when,' and 'when.'"

All these silver waves so welcome to our ear,
Died on the shore of less than half a year.
    One woe is past ; but soon another came :
A week of more intense and awful pain.
Of pain ! but oh ! what sweetness with it blent!
A mingled cup of woe and bliss, not sent
By even shining angels 'round the throne ;
But God's kind l and that chalice brought alone.
'Twas compóunded in His dispensary
When He laid the plan to bring to glory,
Through His own Son, our lost and sinful race:
But e'er unsealed the fountain of His grace,
This bitter cup---yea! only bitter then---
Had to press the lips of the Son of man.
He drank it low in the garden for us,
And He drained it's bitter upon the cross.
    But God filled up from the passion of Christ,
A small cup left for the ransomed to taste.
If we drink in His life's most precious flow,
We "the fellowship of His suff'ring" know.
As afflictions of Christ in us abound,
"So our consolation in Him" is found.
    But the blood that flowed from His sacred feet
Dropped down in our cup a redeeming sweet.

    We suffered in soul, mind, and flesh as well,
But no spirit was there from the shades of hell.

Nay! 'Twas the hand of God alone that pressed
The bliss-mingled pain upon our breast.
One Spirit with our Father's lowly Son,
Who suffers the horror of earthly sin.
One flesh with her whose steps had gone astray,
Broke from the holy law of truth away.
This placed us 'twixt the suff'ring Lamb of God,
And she whose course had waked the chastening **rod.**
And, bound to both the Sufferer and the cause,
We had—through both the sympathetic laws
Of Heav'n above, and earth beneath---to share
The painful wounds that Jesus Christ did bear.
One week the gall of sin, and throes of hell,
For Jesus' sake our lot and portion fell.
A fever caused by soul and mental pains,
Seemed to dry the blood within our veins.
And in this fellowship of Jesus' cup,
Our nervous fluids were so taken up,
That in but one long sleepless parching night
Of inward pain, approved in Heaven's sight,
We felt our hair was surely turning gray,
And found it silvered at the dawn of day.
O! in that furnace of deep heart distress,
God magnified His law of holiness
To our wrought up and fevered mind so high,
That, O my God! it seemed that we must die

At thought of sin, of hers that seemed our own,
She flesh of our flesh, and bone of our bone.
    In this baptism of suffering with Him,
We saw, as ne'er before the curse of sin.
What visions, O thou holy One of Heaven!
In this dark Golgotha hast thou given
Of thy great passion for our sinful race!
O my Lord! Behold the cost of saving grace!
How mean our highest thoughts of Jesus' love!
How slow to learn the woes that sin must prove!
And, Lord! how stupid was our heart to see
Our debt, our boundless debt to thee,
For bearing all our sin's most dreadful load,
And saving us from death and hell's abode:
Until the week we spent with thee alone,
In thy red garden, Calv'ry, and the tomb!
It is enough, O God! Anew I fall
Low in the dust and ashes, and this all
Of life, of soul and body, render up
To Christ, my precious Lord, who drank the cup
Of all my sins, and all the world's beside.
    What e'er of weakness, O thou Crucified!
By grace and former furnace unremoved,--
Thy higher, perfect, standard all approved—
Shall now be purged, O God! to uttermost,
Yea! by thy blood, and by the Holy Ghost.

Thy Sanctifier, Lord! we've owned, and yet
We see the weaknesses that have beset.
And now, O Christ! from this propitious hour,
Thou art our perfect wisdom, peace, and pow'r!
    Then on our heart there came another care.
Our only son, my child! how could I bear
The thoughts of him dissevered from my breast?
By day and night affection's burden pressed.
Though from the time delusion's spell was thrown
'Round that heart, her child no mother's love had
Yet judging from affection's inward glow, [known.
We trowed a mother's heart must ever flow
Toward the lovely product of her womb.
Hence 'twas unkindness we could not presume,
To write and humbly ask the happy gift
Of all on earth that to our heart was left.
Warm love assumed a fever in our breast,
Yet kindly thoughts forbade that we request
A mother to forego that special joy,
Maternal love must find within her boy.
    At last the eye of Him who sees and hears
The restless pangs and groans and midnight tears
Of all His children when by grief oppressed,
Beheld us in paternal love distressed,
Then on our troubles blessed comfort smiled, [child."
Thus saying, "grieve not; for you may have your

For, lo! that heart you thought would feel bereaved,
From mother's care is willingly relieved:
With pure affection 'twere a pleasing toil,
But this expired, it is a drudging moil.
So then we wrote, and this the prompt reply,
"You may come and get the boy for aught care I."
The blessed train that bore us to that son
Seemed that day impatient slow to run.
    We met, and lo! upon his little face
A famine of parental love we trace.
Three days we tarried there with praying much[touch
That God's kind hand once more wife's heart might
With love.   Yea, with one single precious beam
Of affection, where once a living stream
Poured freely forth, to bless our happy home:
But now, alas! congealed in icy zone.
    In vain we wished one moment's private talk:
And last I begged that we together walk
Just outside the city, where lay the dead,
Sleeping silently within their narrow bed.
And where, between two virgil evergreens,
A little mound more dear than any seems:
The grave of our Levella Modest child, [smiled.
On whose sweet brow but three bright summers
She was her mother's idol and first-born,
Her childish virtues mem'ry still adorn.

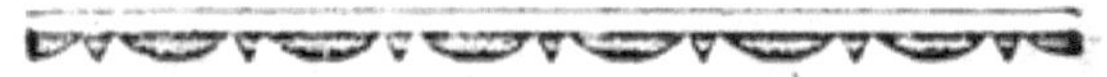

But this request she cooly yet declined,
As if no love to living 'r dead remained.
Then taking that one warm and little hand,
We slowly walked where the cold marbles stand.
'Long the way dear Sidney chatted merrily,
Little knowing what in our bosom lay.
Poor child!   'Twas hard t' respond his prattling
With the tribute of tears that grief affords. [words
God bless the dear boy!   We devoutly pray
That he ne'er may feel what we did that day.
We came to the spot where was laid to rest
The casket cold that was formerly blest
With a pure and lovely spirit bud,
That had gone to bloom in the home of God.
And there by the foot of that little mound,
We kneeled in prayer on the turfy ground.
Dear Sidney—bless the child!—remember how
In fam'ly worship he was want to bow
Close to our side in sweet innocent grace,
So he gently came and resumed his place.
And his tender heart leaped with gladness there,
As his name went up in the breath of prayer.
   But Oh! that hour, what deep emotions rose!
No earthly speech could then our heart disclose.
For our child's dear sake some poor words were used,
But they failed to bear what was inward mused.

O! 'Twas there we longed for the poet's flight,
To sing relief to affection's deep blight.
When emotions rise like a swelling flood,
And submurge the soul, it is then we would
That some kind angel would but lend his harp,
For to start the flow of a sur-charged heart.
But mundane language gave no wings to thought,
And our pensive spirit in tears flowed out.
So the prayer that was for words too deep,
Laid down its burden at the Savior's feet.
Thank God! in that hour to Gethsemane,
Seemed a kind angel come to comfort me,
And the bitter-most cup that could not pass,
Was sweetened by Heavenly love and grace.
  On the morrow early there came a cab,
And a mother's farewell to her bless'd lad.
That parting hour we thought must surely prove,
Some ling'ring traces of a mother's love.
Can she, by nature next to God so dear,
Bid her sweet child adieu without a tear?
Can she ope' the door of maternal fold,
To her own tender flesh of three years old,
And let him fly this darksome world about,
A mother's needed care to do without?
Me thought her heart must sure with anguish swell,
To bid her child, perhaps a last farewell.

But O! our heart was pained, and chilled our blood,
To witness in a jesting laughing mood,
Mother grasp that pure and innocent hand,
And exact of the child this vain demand,
When proudly stepping back into the yard,
"Good by Sidney, write me a postal card?"
    O hath those eyes, with love sparkling once so
Beheld the fabled gorgon's monstrous sight?  [bright,
Which seeing, as the ancient legends run,
Quickly turned its beholder into stone.
    Four years have fled, and yet is frozen up
That heart that was a precious golden cup,
Which once did such nectarian joy afford,
And into which with lavish heart we poured
Every tribute love's magic skill could find,
And mutual reapt the bliss of peace and love combined.
Occasional letters those years gone by,
Breathing words of love that cannot die,
And kindly appeals for her to return,
And wake to her soul's immortal concern,
Elicited naught but silent contempt,
As if they had been to a mummy sent,
Or to one gone down in the valley's gloom,
And had slumbered long in the silent tomb.
Hushed! All hushed! by spiritual death, that hand,
Rusted that pen which cheered this prairie land,

And this burning heart fifteen years ago ;
That heart and ink, frozen, has ceased to flow.
  O God! how vast, how awful now the change !
My startled soul wakes to the fact so strange !
As my feet tread once more this prairie grass,
The varied scenes of fifteen years repass,
Like a panorama before our eyes ;
And our soul, o'erwhelmed in deep surprise,
Is perplexed to know if true—for they seem,
Like eventful years in a passing dream—
Was that angel form an illusion fair ?
And t' weight she left our heart a dark night-mare ?
O ! if such boundless gain and loss were real,
Could fragile human life survive the weal?
Nay, I behold this plain with an actual gaze,
In 'whelming awe admire the sunset blaze.
As falling trees before the mighty gale,
Draw swiftly down to earth their verdant sail,
So I am cast upon this fleecy spot,
By the rushing force and whirl of vivid thought.
And here prostrate, upon this new mown hay,
An humble form, O God! I conscious lie.
*Conscious?* Yes, all that passed before my soul,
Were visions drawn on mem'ry's faithful scroll.
Which by the hand of gracious Providence,
Were wisely folded up, concealed from sense,

Lest hung to view where paths of duty lie,
They'd held our step and dimmed our moisten'd eye.
But on this plain, which so sweetly wears
The 'witching charm of love's two golden years,
The past comes rushing up in mystic flow,
And sets the chanting muses all aglow.
Or, dropping legends of antiquity,
We should more truly and devoutly say;
Not goddess muses touched our mournful lyre;
But the Spirit of Daniel's God did inspire
This humble narrative, in song to trace,
To bless and magnify His wondrous grace.
To this pure object of our simple strain,
May God's effulgent wisdom guide our pen.
    Hear then  as t' hand of Love we greatful trace,
And strain our droning notes to sing His grace.

      Oft we have known the manly breast,
    Where beat a heart of noble cast
    Where temp'rance wrote her righteous code,
    And virtue found a sweet abode.
    And o'er whose pure and peaceful brow,
    Good hope had placed her brilliant bow.
    But Ah! Alas! how changed the scene!
    How short the distance oft between
    The path that shines with virtue bright,

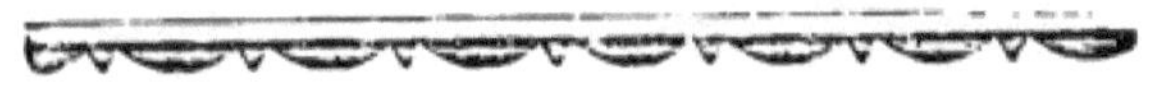

And that o'er cast by sinful night.
The bloom of health has faded from
The cheek;   and now the haggard form
So truly tells the sad sad tale
That cursed whiskey, rum and ale,
Have, serpent like, encoiled the soul.
And blasted by the mad'ning bowl,
The victim reels along the streets,
While pity's eye beholding weeps.
'Till a drunkard's grave for shame cover,
The wreck of what was once a lover,
Which, driven by adverse winds, had struck
Upon some treach'rous hidden rock.
And that love voyage failing port,
His blasted hope yields up the fort,
Casts down her colors in the dirt,
Buries his soul in broken heart.
    And this sad tale we hear recite,
The sequel of love's cruel blight.
From shady grove where met to pray,
The saints upon the Lord's sweet day,
Returned one man with fam'ly kind,
But what, O horror! did they find?
When ent'ring home's endearing fold!
On kitchen floor, there, lifeless, cold,
Lay his son—O pitying God!—

His garments welt'ring in his blood,
In his cold hand lay, tightly grasp'd
The weap'n that ser'e'd his dark behest.
A note was left, we've understood,
That told the cause, and sad prelude
Of that dark shocking tragedy.
And what but blasted love could be
Precursor of that sudden shock,
That from this stage so ruthless shook
That fine youth, and a millstone prest,
Of hopeless grief on father's breast?
And cast a pall of dread amaze
O'er brothers' sisters' future days,
And, methinks, disturbed the bed
Of mother's rest among the dead!
Ah! such and varied scenes unnumbered throng
All the eventful human path along.
This larum then to all we'd loudly sound,
Beware how you tread on love's sacred ground,
Lest from thy tamp'ring forth some tendrils shoot,
And may some guileless heart entwine about.
Which, should'st thou blight and ruthless tear away
May bring, alas! a bleeding mournful day.


We've known in youth what pity took
For human form, but woeful look.

Whose presence might this question call,
Why forced upon this friendless ball,
To take existence without gain?
An unblest and unpitied swain,
Whose only sign of life was—why
He seemed to have a dread to die.
                                    For
"Some men were born for great things,
    And some were born for small,
Some—it is not recorded
    Why they were born at all."—*
    Yet life in him one object lent,
To show the bottomless extent
That men may slide in mortal woes
Who, t'spite a rival, crop their nose.
In a dingy hut and a little town,
Our subject staid, and was its sole renown.
And when losing Powell and missing train,
The burg went back to mother earth again
Ask not how lived the man of wretched fame,
For that's what men could never ascertain.
And some avered he scarcely lived at all,
Save at huskings, raisings, and such like call
Where the poor starved prodigy'd afford
An opportunity at the laden board

*Carleton.

To swallow—not taking time to masticate—
Roasted pig, mutton, poultry, ham and stake,
Bread and potatoes, pie, and fish,
And every welcome large or desert dish.
Whatever happened thence to pass around,
Or sat somewhere within the sweeping bound
Of the poor glutton's palsied raking hand,
Wheeled right and left in line at his command,
Marched up, and greedily were gormandized.
While some forgot to eat, so much surprised,
Others, not restraining flow of humor,
Cracked satiric jests upon that tumor.
*Eating* on the back of that community,
An offence to God, himself and all humanity.
Lashed by the tale of every wit and wag,
Like a green-head on the rump of switching nag.
His raiments in an oily language spoke
That they had never learned the use of soap.
And too plainly by their shreds and flaps declared
That their poor dolesome master roughly fared.
Well! Well! one half his coat-tail's gone astray,
Or both perhaps unkindly torn away,
By wicked hands that made poor John their sport,
And rudely whirled him in the streets about.
He was the butt of every trick and game,
Of wit's ingenious quip, and buffoon's shame.

Upon his back the snick'ring laughing crew
Adroitly placed some tag or scand'lous cue,
Or hung, as an extension of his spine,
The last, long, caudal end of some old swine.
When children wished on others spite to vent,
"Old P.'s" name was the ugliest thing they sent.
Vermin cursed his pallet's greasy rags,
While night and day, were only heavy drags,
That irksome bore upon his lifeless life ;
For old dame misery was his bosom wife.
He'd won another, but by death rivaled,
His bleeding heart in deep sorrow struggled,
'Till heard and sanctioned this dark spirit's voice,
"Madam Misery is my second only choice."
　　So he courted and hugged her ghostly form,
And he drank from her cup a life forlorn.
He wished not even one short honey-moon,
Despair hung o'er his days her sable gloom.
Not a smile ever lit his stolid mein ;
For his life throughout was a cheerless dream.
He chose it so.　Far round him shone in youth,
Every beaming and cheerful hope.　In truth
His name once wore bright honor and respect,
And no mean store had decked his intellect.
　　But what adverse fate. Ah ! need you yet ask ?
Spread over his life its deadly blast !

What woeful cloud eclipsed a hope so fair,
And congealed that heart in blank despair?
What drove poor Johnny from the happy plain,
Of social dignity, to the hermit's den?
'Twas the crisis of disappointed love.
That so darksomely drew our sketch above.
    And now our song at last has reached the place
Where our spirit would try its debt of grace
To pay to Him whose mighty arm sustained,
Our bleeding heart, while its cup of grief we drained:
That life and peace's prolonged, and even joy,
And holy comfort, which to quite destroy,
Apolyon's host had plotted fiendish well.
But disappointed, writhing, back to hell
They take their course, amazed at Heaven's power,
To sustain a soul in the furious hour.
O God! this heart, where love so warmly glows,
And its return such blessed rapture knows,
And where afflictions long in youth had past,
And wrought a nervous melancholy cast,
Heart to affection's wound so sensative!
O! can there in this smoking flax survive,
Unquenched, the flame of life, and bow of hope?
But for thy grace, O Lord! might we not grope
In the shadows that hung more black than death.
Where inward grief tolls out each mournful breath,

From a heart amazed by sorrow into stone,
A dead spirit chained in a living tomb?
O God! but for thy arm unseen on earth,
This fragile form might even curse its birth,
  And sit, dark brooding, trembling where
  Some dingy hut shut out the gaze
  Of human eye, and orient blaze;
  Forced only from that drear abode,
  By hunger's sharp resistless goad;
  Then quailing with unmanly dread,
  The noise of fellow human's tread.
  Or, unsupported by that love
  That flows direct from Him above,
  When the conjugal, next in pow'r,
  Was ruthless torn in peril's hour,
  Perhaps, to drown such bitter grief,
  We might have rushed upon the reef
  Of liquor's black infernal spell,
  And hastened quickly down to hell.
  Or, life surviving hope, had pressed
  Too heavy on a Christless breast,
  To 'bide the time that's made by rum,
  Which takes on board a hell begun,
  And had taken up the fatal line,
  Around the capstan to entwine,
  The end flung on a pile secure,

On 'ternity's unwelcome shore,
The voyage end, by demon's sport,
In suicidal's horrid port.
No eye but thine, O Deity!
Can see what end of misery,
What horrid black and cursed fate,
Might have cast its crushing weight,
Upon this helpless bruised reed,
Did not thy comforts far exceed
The highest billows earth may roll
O'er a grace-clad and ransomed soul!


Hallelujah! here our pent up gratitude,
Upwelling must break forth in praise to God.
O where, on all this blood and tear-drenched clod,
Is there such help as found in Israel's God?
Such succor in the hour of fell distress,
As leaning hard upon His faithfulness?
Let not the lucrative boast in their wealth,
Nor the strong and vigorous trust in health.
Such god's lift high thy supercilious crest,
Inflate with self-sufficiency thy breast.
But when misfortunes meet thee in the way;
Thy gold has fled, or mortal powers decay,
Thy child is dead, or bosom love is turned to gall,
Then on your gods, ye fools in vain may call.

They answer but in ashes on thy head,
And, lo! mocking thy calamity, are fled.
Nor yet recumbent on thy treasures digged in schools
From whence too often, wisdom aping fools
Go forth great pompous, self-conceited mud,
And totally eclipse the light of God.
　　"Then, lest religion they should need,
　　Of pious Hume they learn their creed,
　　By strongest demonstrations shown,
　　Evince that nothing can be known.
　　Take arguments unmixed by doubt
　　On Voltaire's trust. or go without,
　　'Gainst Scriptures rail in modern lore,
　　As thousand fools have railed before."—*
What have ye then for all your folly's pain,
Who fret. and work. exhume. and search in vain,
To rid thy conscience of thy Maker's laws,
And rob good sense and nature of her cause?
Preferring for thy sire the stupid ape,
E'er confessing Him who only can create.
And deify, instead, unbridled lust,
Doubt Heaven's truth, but freely hell intrust.
Boast of free thought. while yet a menial slave
To thy depraved and beastly passion's rave.
And, as though reason can't with virtue blend,

*JOHN TRUMBULL.

Ye sin-perverted loud its light pretend.
If wisdom's province were to serve the devil,
Then could ye skeptics prove your heads were level.
    What compensation hath the scoffer's cant?
What good remunerates his churlish rant?
Where's thy blind reason gone when troubles roll
Like billows dark o'er thy distracted soul?
Where, Ah! where is thy boasted fortitude,
When fled away some doted earthly good?
When death hath torn away thy cherished ones,
Or wedded love to rival's bosom turns?
Then what's thy carping jest of sacred things?
What comfort to a stricken spirit brings
Thy proud conceit begotten unbelief
Of God, the only true and blest relief
A soul can find in sorrow's starless night,
When sweetest dearest hopes are struck with blight?
O God! how oft neglected and denied
Art thou, in hearts deceived by foolish pride;
Until that smarting rod, adversity,
Teaches fools, who will learn no other way,
Their need of thee Most High, who formed the breast,
To calm it's heaving troubles into rest.
    And ye mad, frenzied on politic gods,
Who fuss and wrangle for your demagogues;
Why to them caters, unrequited tools,

With that high fevered zeal that only cools,
When 'lections end in rival party's crow,
And all your faces sullen lengthy grow,
Crest fallen, dark, dejected and would sour?
What profit have you, when returns devour
Thy boasted, wagered, hope of victory?
Laughed, and jeered, and gibed, this thy only pay.
　But if good fortune turn upon thy side,
And thy idol be to office deified,
What blessing then calls forth thy boist'rous swells?
Ye crazed, who hoarse your throats with fiendish yells,
And make night frantic with your din of horns,
Or louder yet, blow off your head or arms,
With powder's fool destroying crippling blast?
Hath that strained vote thy vaunted party cast
Released thy soul from sin, remorse and hell?
That ye such weird midnight orgies swell?
Hath the election of thy candidate
Elected thee to Heaven's tranquil state?
Or is it to thy soul a guarantee
That thou shalt from the ills of life be free?
Will the horn-of-plenty henceforth overflow
With a more lavish harvest where ye sow?
Will thy champion's mace vouchsafe protection
'Gainst social and domestic disaffection?
Or be a present help in time of need?

A panacea for wounds that smart and bleed?
And will he soothe and bind thy breaking-heart,
When from thy stricken bosom loved ones part?
Or should treachery, deep and black as hell,
Invade thy home and cast her blighting spell
O'er the one that so electrified thy life,
And woe succeed the blessings of a wife;
Will then thy chosen hero to thee fly,
If thou, in thy bitterest grief shouldst cry
To his lordship, when thy wild mournful strain
Trembles on the verge of a maddened brain?
And if coming, hath he that magic power;
To dispel the grief-clouds that o'er thee lower:
Can he tune again thy unstrung manhood?
And drive from thy spirit sorrow's dark brood
Of spectres round thee gathered, fierce as hell,
Holding to thy fevered brain a picture, fell,
Of eternal vengeance, 'till thy blood boil
With red retaliation's murdrous spoil?
Or on thy musing spirit mocking stare,
The gastly forms of blackness and despair,
'Till life is shrouded in a hopeless night.
And grows a curse too great for human might,
Which, bidding high for earth's commiseration,
Buys it dear in hell's precipitation?
   O ye gods of pride, gold, and infidelity,

Of science, honor, and of rivalry.
Yea! all ye midnight gods of secrecy,
And stupid sectish gods of bigotry,
All, and every god by men and devils formed,
Of objects real, or by fancy's call suborned,
Ye are but subtile cheats, and worthless trash,
And all your devotees are blind and rash.
All gog and magog deities combined,
Cannot repletely fill one hungry mind.
O were ye potent more than ancient stones,
To meliorate the wounds around your thrones,
Were ye worth a farthing in the hour of grief,
Or could but drop on pain one olive leaf.
Then would not from your daily presses rise
A stygian smoke of news that black the skies.
Then too would not your crimson colums drip
With human gore from every measured stick.
The crimes and woes that groan upon your sheets,
Prove that ye, of life and happiness, are cruel cheats.
A banker fails, and takes his drooping life;
A merchant next, and trouble spectres, rife,
Rushing on his melancholic mind,
Around his neck the fatal rope entwined.
　A Lutheran farmer, earthly well to do,
Lost his health, with it manly prestige too.
And, knowing not the God of consolation,

Could not endure the petty imputation
Of looking well, and yet to work unable.
So from a rafter in his 'pienished stable,
Swung down himself into eternity.
Sad comment on our poor humanity.
So weak without the Author of our being,
From dim shadows into blackness fleeing.
    And, here following in the doleful train,
This very day the current news proclaim
An eastern man of prominence insane,
For which the late elections have the blame.
    We passed a farm of rich productive soil,
Where wealth had freely blessed the owner's toil.
His fields were large, his buildings all in taste,
But the proud farmer was of skeptic cast.
All his conversation well evinced that he
To gods of lucre only bowed the knee.
The God he had so madly disavowed,
Whose hand of mercy had his life endowed,
Allowed a sudden and a fearful storm,
Whose resistless pathway coursed his farm.
One barn was damaged, some fruit trees perished,
When fled the worthless gods his heart had cherished.
The foolish man arraigned himself before
The bar of his own conscience, charged with more
Than his blind reason counsel could defend.

And, eager the perplexing suit should end,
Christ, the only potent Advocate, renounced,
And this rash verdict on himself pronounced,
That by his willing hands he must despoil
The citadel of life in hempen coil.
For his life—reduced by sin to idle sport—
The man made no appeal to higher court,
But, weary of his soul's remorseful dirth,
'Reft of hope, took his exit from the earth.
    But why pursue the dismal scene,
    Of living ghosts that haunt the spleen
    Of human life, from Him astray,
    Whose smile alone can bless the day
    When sorrows roll like billows high,
    And disappointments shroud the sky!
    Then boasted human energy,
    With all your fickle comforts flee.
    The schemes on which your lives are **spent**
    Are worthless;   and but discontent,
    And gloom, spread o'er your wretched **souls,**
    Attracted by such treach'rous poles.
        When petty griefs that life attend,
    On thy sick heart their arrows spend,
    Your man-hood sinks, your heads are **crazed,**
    Or self destruction ends your days.
    But th' greater curse of treachery,

That wakens green-eyed jealousy,
More certain still this sequel brings,
As poet Rogers briefly sings.
"She loved another, love was in that sigh?
On the cold ground he throws himself to die."
Or murder takes its alternate,
In seducer or the victim's fate.
　　But 'neath the reign of Heaven's love,
How sweetly, and how blest we prove
That balm the Prince of Peace bestows,
When deepest wound of sorrow flows.
Ah! then, exceeding joyful in
Our tribulation's deepest sting.
O! when our greatful heart rejoiced,
And o'er flowed in praises voiced,
Then flashed this thought in rapt surprise,
Which,—pausing speech, with weeping eyes —
We thus exclaimed;　"O Gracious Heav'n!
Can to this potsherd yet be giv'n
Such boundless sweet felicity,
Despite our great calamity?
Can grace transmute to sweetness all
Graceless hearts most bitter call?
'Tis even so, O righteous God!
What glory yields thy chast'ning rod!
Where all the gods of earth and air,

Forsake their dupes to wild despair,
Is thy provident occasion
To raise thy saints t' nobler station.
And that which crushes "sons of men,"
Us lifts the star of Bethlehem,
And opens wide the gates of praise,
Yea! tunes our soul to sweeter lays.


Sins greatly callous hearts and petrify,
And all man's finer feelings stupefy.
So hearts debased by sin and lustful lords,
Have 'laxed and paralyzed affection's ch rds,
And rendered sentient souls insensitive.
To wounds of love the sanctified receive.
So holy hearts do feel a thousand fold
More deeply the stings of broken love than cold
And heartless sinners can, whose half congealed
Affections far less happy transports yield,
And are much less capable of pain;
For life, when elevated to a higher plain
Enlarges its susceptibility
Both to grief, and raptures of felicity.
The fruitage most delicious and mature,
Bruise more easily than the hard and sour.
The flow'rs that are most pleasing, sweet and rare,
Unto the eye most beautiful and fair,

And that do most delicious odors give,
Are to the sting of frost most sensitive.
The sinner's nature, gross and hard and blind,
Is dead to many pains that hearts refined,
And blest with higher life in Christ endure.
But, Alas! dead likewise to all t' pure
Eternal joys that flood the heart enshrined
With Jesus Christ, His peace, and heav'nly **mind.**
He is oblivious to that holy love,
That 'quaints us with the bliss enjoyed above.
Dead to all true objects of a human soul,
A planet wand'ring from its orb and pole.
   So while increase of life involves some pain,
Its sphere enlarged, enhances all our gain.
Who'd amputate a strong and healthy limb,
Lest mosquitoes on it light and sting?
Or who dethrone his noble intellect,
Because some mental griefs we may expect?
If animal and mental life's prized so high,
Why leave your soul so dead and stupid lie?
'Tis sad to look upon the lifeless clay,
More melancholy yet the mind's decay,
But. O the soul! the actual "inward man!"
More awful still its death, beneath the ban
Of sin, and burning lust's malignant spell,
And trembling, guilty, on the verge of hell.

All glory be to Heaven's matchless grace!
O Christ! our Everlasting life and peace!
Thou art in us a bright illumination
Of body, mind, soul : an inspiration
That sings happy over death and the tomb,
Carries away the pall of mental gloom,
Bursts the narrow shell of soul-ignorance,
Lifts the incubus, and breaks t' dismal trance
Of sin, that chained the wretched spirit fast,
In the vile dungeon, whence by satan cast.
Thou, Great Deliv'rer! hast flung wide t' prison,
And our dreamy souls, by thy touch 'risen,
Now go forth, blest with freedom evermore,
From the cell of sin, in worlds of light t' soar.
The soul exults with rapture as she doth
View t' blazing glory of Eternal Truth.
And, by telscope of Heav'ns inspiration,
Such bright beams of majestic wisdom shine,
Beholds, throughout redemption's new creation,
Such heighths,depths, lengths, and breadths of love
That she expands 'till true to Bible adage, [Divine,
She knows the love of God that passeth knowledge.
Thus, uncaged, winged aloft in realms of light,
We take vastly wider ranges of delight,
And drink in pleasures manifold increas'd.
While from earthly pains and griefs we're released.
By grace and glory, that so freely stream

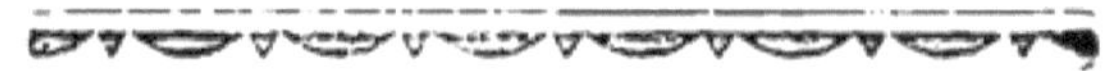

Direct from Heav'n and sweetly supervene
In sorrow, a joy so inexpressible,
That e'en pain, for Christ's sake, is pleasurable.
    Happy the people who such bliss afford!
Yea! happy they whose God is Christ the Lord!
Ten thousand thanks we pour low at the feet
Of Love Supreme, and Wisdom so complete,
That over ruled the gates of hell, for-sooth,
Conspired 'gainst a feeble lover of the truth.
    No other furnace could have proved so great,
None other threatened with such awful fate,
And yet no ordeal, but this whitened flame,
So placed us on the overcomer's plain.
So the storm of black satanic fury,
God has turned to songs of endless glory.
    Not on that loved one hell's game chiefly turned,
But 'twas on this dust his ire so hotly burned.
Nor cared he yet so much to sink our soul,
As to hush the thunders of that "flying roll."
While our soul's escaped to higher summit,
And light and Truth ir marching on so blessed,
Tis sad that one who proved so great a profit,
Both in love's fruition, and its painful forfeit,
D inks not with us, at the crystal river,
That makes glad the City of God forever.
But, brother! blame her not, we humbly ask.

Nor on her cherished bosom ruthless cast
One vindictive thought. or word, or frown.
But, as Christians, let us bow and truly own
That Providence, which seems to fall severe
On some souls, others to refine more clear.
The ill, charge to satan, and ourself include,
The good ascribe, with humble gratitude,
To Him that kindly doeth all things well,
And frustrates all the wicked plots of hell.
Yea! if any but the devil be to blame,
By God's grace we will assume the shame.
For had not satan found us so. o'er lent
On her, he might have ne'er conceived t' intent.
He saw us holding childlike to her gown,
And judged her fall would likewise cast us down.
And well he judged;   for e'er released our grasp,
Our soul was mid the fiends of darkness cast.
Yea! satan saw in our confiding weakness,
A chance to sink our soul in sorrow's hopeless.
But God likewise, observed the situation,
Saw how to magnify His great salvation.
    Salvation! Ah! yes Lord! that tells it all.
That magic word sweets the bitterest gall.
The gold that's wrapped within its secret folds
Redeemed this tested being from the mould.
Salvation hath reserved a charm for life.

Without which all, *all*, wou'd have fled with wife.
  O Sarah! once within this breast of mine,
All joy and bliss arose and fell with thine.
Life's sunshine sparkled in thy lovely lips,
My spirit's light went out with thy eclipse.
It seemed the throbbing of this very heart
Must die if it from thine be torn apart.
That life could only linger in this breast
While it conjointly with thine own was blest.
Ah! did I think that blood could warm this frame
If thou shouldst live, and yet oar lives be twain!
Or were not earth a cold and dismal wild,
If thy love-star no longer on it smiled!
That gorgeous Sun, me thought, could shed no cheer,
Should its dull rays e'er fall upon, my dear!
An ice-wall risen up between our hearts;
Nor spread his pleasing dyes as day departs.
Could even spring, the verdant time of love,
Within our heart one sweet emotion move,
Should e'er its music fall upon our ears,
Unmingled with thy love of former years?
Or could the summer's golden glory smile,
Or Autumn's tinted picture yet beguile,
Or Winter's merry chime, and silver frost
Tinge the clouds of woe that would o'er cast
Our mournful sky, me thought, if life be left,

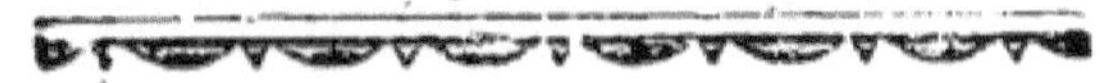

And yet that life of all thy love bereft!
  But, Ah! dear Lord! in wonder we confess
Thy grace and love excelled our highest guess.
 For, lo! my single path is set along
With gems of bliss that tune my soul to song.
Salvation gilds my days with richer gold,
And all the scenes of earth and Heav'n unfold
In holy joy, compelling us to own
That life, bereft of all but God alone.
May, with His own precious self and love enshrined,
Exceed the glory of His gifts combined.


  So we beg the readers of this story—
Attuned to sing the Eternal glory
Of grace Divine—Yea! exact this pledge of you,
Drop no blame on her we've known in love so true.
  We have suffered much.—But O the precious gain!
She more, in the loss of that which suffers pain.
The dying of those chords of fine sensation,
That vibrate to the touch of pure affection;
And yet, withal, inflict such cruel pain,
And bleed our hearts when love takes an averse vein.
O what misfortune can excel the dread
Of a heart where love-chords are cold and dead!
O! if needs be, let this heart in sorrow bleed,
This were, we hold, a blessing sweet indeed,

Compared with this, the death of that which knows
The wounds of love, and also that bestows
The boon of pure and sweet angelic bliss,
When its fervent beams hearts united bless.
These love-tendrils, make music yet within,
In hallowed consolation ever bring
Sweet recollections of loves golden hours,
While I alone, in memory tread her bowers.
This joy remains us, to love her yet withal,
Better unrequited love than none at all.


What then?   Shall life move down a cheerless
Our fellows only meeting to complain        [lane,
Of our sad lot, more than by death bereft?
As if no solace to a soul were left
When all created bliss had taken wings,
And when dried up this earth's refreshing springs.
Ah! no, there's yet a stream in which to bathe
The fevered mind and lonely breast; a wave
That sings upon the troubled shores of time,
A song of love that greets this soul of mine,
And charms to silence every inward wail,
And cheers my pilgrimage up through the vail;
So all my troubles are forgotten here below.
What can I wish? O God! thy overflow
Of love and grace and peace have shut my mouth,

And my heart beguiled from every thought of drouth.
Shall I then chatter like the swallow here,
And thus draw out the sympathetic tear?
Or wince for pities from my fellows round?
What for? Behold! such joy and peace abound
That life, in spite of hell, is all replete.
Nay, let me rather offer at thy feet
The service of my busy life to bear
Thy words of comfort to the hearts of care.
To administer the soothing lotion
To others, rather than excite compassion.
The world is full of hearts in grief oppressed;
Send us with balm for every wounded breast.
'Tis far more blest to give a cheerful smile,
And some beclouded soul from doubts beguile,
Than receive a thousand kind condolences
For woes the grace of God out balances.


Now shall my heart more joyfully ascend
To God, where all our aspirations end.
Cleansed by blood, by furnace still more purified,
Shines His Spirit in our heart a perfect guide.
All our happy being into holier air,
Like an angel strong, He doth so sweetly bear;
Where earthly passion-clouds have no abode,
But mind, soul, body, all are swallowed up in God.

Forever, O my precious Lord! I am thine,
More than ever thine, a living shrine,
Of thy fulness, Father, Spirit, Son.
O Thou Blessed, Eternal Three in One!

                         Amen!

# SOUL-CRIPPLE CITY.

THE plan of this poem was suggested to our mind by E. E
Hasty's tract, entitled "Soul-cripple Island." We preferred to
use a City, because the Scriptures illustrate the medley of sect-
ism by the City of Babylon.

Beecher is represented as having said, "The human soul is
lame, and Christianity gives it crutches." That is a pretty fair
representation of sect religion. The deceiver has kept the eyes
of her devotees from the recreating and healing power of the
Gospel of Christ, and upon the pernicious crippling sect props.
The Church is compared to the perfect human body;
and what crutches are to a sound man, sect institutions are to
the real Church the complete body of Christ, and the same arguments will apply to either. The idea of wooden crutches being a constituent part of our physical structure is no more ridic-
ulous than that sect incorporations are essential parts of the
Church.

"As if the staff should lift itself up, as if it were no wood."—
Isa 10: 15.

"Lo thou trustest in the staff of this broken reed, on Egypt;
whereon if a man lean, it will go into his hand, and pierce t."
—Isa. 36: 6.

"My people ask counsel at their stocks, and their staff declareth unto them. * * * They have gone a w oring  om under their God."—Hosea, 4: 12.

"How is the strong staff broken, and the beautiful rod!"—
Jer. 48: 17.

"The Lord hath broken the staff of the wicked."—Isa, 14: 5.

These passages are certainly to be taken in a spiritual sense
and they show God's abhorrence of all props and substitutes that
men invent, found and lean upon, instead of simply "staying on
God in truth," leaning all on Christ, and abiding in the one
divine Body, the Church.

# SOUL-CRIPPLE CITY.

NOT a mere imaginary
    Object, born on fancy's wing,
Is the city of this story,
    But a real historic thing.
  Though by tropes and proper figures
    We delineate her fame,
  Though she has some mystic features,
    She's an entity the same.


She's a city, but not local,
    A disorder wide diffused,
Or a system-cursed confusion,
    By each system more confused.
So we'll briefly trace her hist'ry,
    And inspect her filthy streets,
Taking disinfectives plenty,
    For the morbidness she keeps.

In the book of Revelation,
    And in prophesy we learn,
An apostate generation
    From the truth astray would turn.
Would forsake the Holy City
    Wherein dwelleth righteousness,
And from Zion's mount of beauty,
    Wander in the wilderness.

And, like Cain who slew his brother,
    Fled into the land of Nod,
From the country of his father,
    "From the presence of his God,"
And there builded him a city,
    These apostates from the Lord,
Were to think them wise and mighty,
    Far above the written Word.

So of them it was predicted,
    That a city they'd devise,
And her deeds so foul and wicked,
    Were to reach unto the skies.
Also these "molten founders"—*
    An insult to Wisdom's Son—
Were to call their bedlams churches.
    But God named her "Babylon."

*Jer. 10: 14

'Tis fulfilled.   They've built the babel
    On the sands of sectish strife.
Her chief founder was the devil,
    Though disguised, she is his wife.
Filth and all abominations
    Lodge in her these latter days.
Her six hundred babel nations
    Tread six hundred crooked ways.

Each one leads direct to heaven,—
    So the bigots all declare—
If you'll take the sectish leaven,
    And each quarter pay your fare.
'Neath a great and tow'ring steeple,
    At the head of every street,
There the mixed and "mingled people,"
    Both to play and worship meet.

There they throng to sell and gamble,
    Crying, "all done, twice and thrice."
Souls are bartered for a trifle,
    Trifles bring the highest price.
There are ladies sold at auction,
    To the highest bidding fool.
Money is the mighty unction,
    That inspires the pulpit tool.

So a thousand shoddy trinkets,
    Dolls and monkeys, pop and ale,
Make the merchandise of babel,
    And insure a pious sale;
For in buying every member
    Gets a ticket he conceits,
That will pass the door of heaven,
    And secure the highest seats.

There are shows and lewd carousals,
    Where the members whoop and laugh,
And with wicked men and devils,
    Dance around the golden calf.
Most conspicuous in the revel,
    Is the hypocritic priest
Who thus serves the very devil,
    'Neath the livery of Christ.

Now they stand in line of battle,
    Mimic war, and muster brooms:
For their pastor's bread and butter,
    They must soften to buffoons.
"Shoulder arms", "there, hold them level"—
    Even women take a part--
"Broom brigades" won't sweep the devil
    Nor his cobwebs out their heart.

New inventions, strange and silly
    Always find a ready sale.
Money begging without scruple,
    Please the prophets, "head and tail."
So they welcomed in the devil,
    Heard him lie to gender fun,
Put him up and sold at auction,
    Just to help the cause along.

How it did surprise the devil.
    That the cripples bid so fast.
All the town was in a rival,
    Nick to have at any cost.
As the sale ran high and rapid,
    Satan hollowed loud and gruff,
"We have legions for your market,
    And you all can have enough.

So the prince of diabolians
    Took the undisguised control;
For he needed now no longer
    Wear a mask in Cripple-Soul.
To his children who could enter
    Only in the rear by stealth,
Now the gateway standeth open,
    If they'll only bring their pelf.

Note that heard and tell, if able,
    Which are sheep, and which are goats,
It would even puzzle Gabriel
    To assort them by their notes.
Why should sheep, if any present,(?)
    All adopt the goatish bleat?
Playing goat will not be pleasant
    At the final judgment seat.


Well denominated babel,
    Such she is in very deed,
A confused and drunken revel,
    Killing souls for mammon greed.
Yet we've named her by Soul Cripple,
    A cognomen justly due.
And you'll set it to her credit
    As her customs we review.

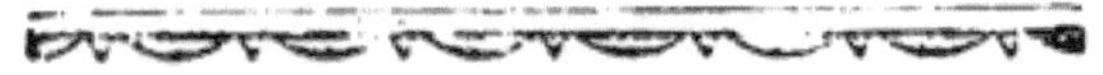

## ALL GO ON CRUTCHES IN CRIPPLE-SOUL.

But whereunto shall we liken,
　Or with what similitude,
Paint this foolish generation?
　Foolish children, sinful brood!
All within that mystic city
　Walk not upright on their feet
But on crutches play the cripple,
　'Tis a custom they must keep.

Not a man in all Soul-Cripple,
　Not a woman, girl or boy,
But must go it on quadruple,
　Must the wooden legs employ.
Not one ever tried it walking
　On created feet alone,
Not on crutches to be stalking
　Were a scandal to the town.

Strength and speed their limbs are losing,
　Although God had made them sound.
But for want of proper using,
　Hang they limpsy to the ground.
Their backs are bent, and shoulders gibbous,
　Thus they mope as quadrupeds.
So agreed it is, there happens
　Some collide protruding heads.

But why go they thus a hobbling,
    Rich and poor, and young and old,
On their wooden members shuffling?
    That's the right way, they are told.
From that city's first conception,
    There went forth a firm edict,
None in her municipation
    Dare in soundness walk erect.

So they hold the old tradition,
    As a law in Cripple Soul.
Each succeeding generation
    Muster crutches in the roll,
Early teach the stupid notion
    To their children as divine,
On their stilted locomotion
    Make them cripple into line.

Now the useless legs they're sporting
    Are of varied stamp and kind,
Each one takes his own assorting,
    To the fancy of his mind.
O'er six hundred fact'ries humming
    Keep the market in supply.
All in competition running,
    All in style and numbers vie.

The oldest crutches in the market
  Are the Roman Papal brand.
They in human blood are painted,
  And the highest price command.
All these antiquated relics
  Bear inscription, Nicene date
And a trademark, dame of harlots,
  Myst'ry babylon the great.

This firm held exclusive patent,
  And monopolized the trade
For twelve hundred years unrivaled,
  Until Luther haply made
The discov'ry that their charter
  Was without authentic seal.
So he blazed abroad the matter
  By his thunder and his quill

Many cast the bloody crutches
  From their galled arms away.
Then an angel held dispatches,
  Feignedly a son of day.
And he hailed the reformation,
  Bid them quickly organize:
Mostly on the old foundation,
  Built they Luth'ran crutcheries.

This is now the eldest daughter
  Of the harlot mother great.
Oath bound prison, souls to slaughter,
  Cursed and degenerate.
And her trade-mark is the second
  Two-horned beast that did appear,
Speaking like unto a dragon.
  And a foaming keg of beer.


Next appeared the English crutches,
  And the High Episcopal.
Thence the mania fast increases,
  Every style conceivable.
Wycliffe crutches, Calvin crutches,
  Quaker, Shaker, Mennonite,
Wesley crutches, in twelve branches,
  M. E. crutches, black and white.


Methodism, Afric, German,
  Methodism Protestant,
Methodism labeled "Calvin,"
  Both M. E's. north and southern brand.
"Free" and "Union" Methodism,
  And the ism "Primitive."
All these horns of beast division,
  On their stilted crutches live.

A dozen clan of Metholism
  Crying here is Christ, and there.
All in lively opposition,
  Compass earth to sell their ware.
Entertain the base and funny,
  Lie and steal, to pious end.
Any rook to raise the money,
  That's the way to raise the wind.

In the nude, and lude and dev'lish
  Metholism takes the sway.
Steeple-houses tall and stylish,
  Mesh and milk the goats to pay.
Festive "tables full of vomit"
  Is the trade-mark of this name.
She's a black and smoking comet,
  And her glory is her shame.

Then there are Baptist crutches,
  Hard-shell, and inflexible.
"Free-will" Baptist, Bond-will Baptist,
  and the creed "Six Principle."
There are Baptist called "Ephrata,"
  Saturnarian Baptist too.
"Anabaptist," and some later
  Baptist crutches we'll undo.

First there are the tri-crutched baptist,
    Three-dip Dunkers, new and old,
"Primitive," "Progressive," factions,
    All spewed out, "twice dead" and cold.
They believe in three immersions,
    Rising filthy from the flood,
But think not of one submersion,
    Neath the precious cleansing blood


In this mart of vain religions
    You will find on Water street,
And at all her river stations,
    Crutches vaunted as complete.
But the clubs that they are vending,
    Are as hollow as a horn :
They that buy need no repenting,
    In cold water they are born.


All that ride upon their notion,
    Think they're valiant in dispute;
Water, river, lake and ocean,
    Here salvation they impute.
"Deny the power" and take our patent,
    Come and join our empty wells.
Note our trade-mark, 'tis a camel
    Feeding empty oyster shells.

Satan cooped a reformation
  In the key-stone-land of Penn.
Eldershipped it, with ovation,
  Down the river to this den.
In the harbor of Soul-cripple,
  Cast her anchor in the mud,
On her main-mast hung the devil
  The misnomer, "Church of God."

Here she places on the market
  Her new crutch in Cripple Soul.
Fills the measure of a bigot,
  In the sacred name she stole.
Her weak crutch is highly varnished,
  And her trade-mark is a cloak,
With a name in amber tarnished,
  And a camp befogged with smoke.

Then she raked the earth for money
  To erect a factory,
In the gassy town of Findlay,
  Where her preacher dudes could be
Taught to ape and mimic others,
  Over nicely mince and nod.
So they dote upon their Athens,
  She's their pride inflating god.

All these bapto 'sociations
    Have a god of water made,
Leaving fire and salvation,
    And the blood without the trade.
More than all the sect who clamor
    Just to make the sinner wet,
Who have swallowed down a Campbell
    And are straining at a gnat.


True, to follow Christ's example
    Is sublime, and very good.
But to dip a trembling sinner,
    Is to set at naught the blood.
Dead to sin and self forever,
    We immerging, testify,
But to plunge and raise a rebel,
    Is to dip him in a lie.


While a drop or two to sprinkle,
    That is but a popish rite,
Catered to the flesh and devil;
    Born in superstition's night.
Yet the drop betrays its meaning,
    Snapped into the sinners face,
That on sponsors he is leaning,
    Hoping for a drop of grace

Since to bury in immersion
    Presupposes we are dead,
Then repent and get salvation
    E'er into the stream you're led.
But if candidate is filthy,
    And to sin he will not die,
Then the smallest bit of water
    Will but tell the lesser lie.

O! ye Presbyterian crutches,
    All of dozy timber made,
"English," "German." "Kirk of Scotland,"
    "Cumberland," "Associate."
And "seceders" from the Bible,
    "Covenanters" and Reformed;
Each priestism is a charnel,
    And your wooden legs deformed.

There are props United Brethren,
    All disjointed out of Christ,
Glassite, Hicksite, and Socinian,
    Rotten Universalist.
There are crutches labeled Christian,
    All the better to deceive:
And an earth-born "Christian Union,"
    That would all together weave.

Materialistic crutches
　　Also occupy a stand.
And some tables spread with clutches,
　　Hop as devils play their hand.
There are crutches Unitarian,
　　Omish, dull of sale and rust.
Also Supralapsitarian,
　　A few Landisites in dust.


There are crutches "Congregational,"
　　And "Associate Reform."
And all dark "Evangelical,"
　　God-forsaken and forlorn.
River Brethren, Shaw's young Missiou,
　　Unswathed, out of season born.
All the bundles we can't mention,
　　A confusion multiform

## MILLER'S NO-SOUL EDITION.

'Twas in eighteen four and forty,
    William Miller set the day,
That he would, with all his party,
    Spread his wings and fly away.
So they robed themselves all ready,
    And assembled in the town.
Though their faith was strong, yet steady
    Gravitation held them down.

As the sun his race was running,
    All with upward gazing eye,
Waited for the Savior's coming,
    To confirm the prophet's lie.
But their flapping was a failure.
    O'er them waned the evening light,
Leaving all the dupes of Miller
    In confusion's darkest night.

But they'd started out to travel
    On some new discovered route,
So, assisted by the devil,
    They must never turn about.
Then they met in general council
    For to hit upon a creed,
Which of all the lies in Cripple,
    Their's must take the very lead.

So the devil searched the record
    Of the meanest lies he'd thought,
Then he moved, and Miller second,
    And 'twas carried by vote;
"These two crutches, in Soul-Cripple
    We will place upon the roll,
That 'neath Sinai we must tremble,
    And deny we have a soul."

Then this craft, in falsehood shapen,
    And conceived in very sin,
Their infernal business open,
    And to bondage gather in.
Use the law to fill their coffers,
    And to spread their lies abroad.
At salvation they are scoffers,
    Keeping Saturday's their god.

But the city council issued
    An injunction on their trade,
For that market, 'twas decided,
    Just for Cripple Soul was made.
O ye Advents ye can never
    In this market hold a stall,
From Soul-Cripple you must sever,
    For ye have no soul at all.

Then the foolish Millerism
   Fell to looking very brown:
Having pitched so far from Zion
   Were not fit for Cripple Town.
So they made a new edition
   In the "wilderness of sin,"
There to vend their blue religion,
   And to spread their legal gin.

'Twas a waste and desert region,
   Once possessed by Sadducees,
Who denied both soul and angel,
   For the fleshly mind to please.
So did Ebionites inhabit
   This parched wild in later years.
In the smoke of burning Horeb,
   There they groped in legal fears.

They were "wanting understanding,
   "Poor in sense," Origen said.
The epistles all rejecting,
   On the pentateuch they stood.
The Galatians were so lawish
   Once to think of moving there,
But the 'postle cried, ye "foolish,"
   Flee from that satanic snare.

So these tramontanian deserts
  Lay for many ages waste,
Till the Non-soul-legal-ventists
  Out of Cripple Soul were cast.
Here in "blackness and the tempest,"
  And beneath the thundering curse,
All these bondage sons of Hagar
  Gathered up their babel force.


Here they walled about their region,
  To exclude all angels' stroll,
And so fear all apparitions
  That they carnify the soul.
And, lest God should make them trouble,
  Say they're only flesh and wind,
Knowing he will never bother
  With the lower cattle kind.

## BOOTH'S ALL NOISE EDITION

Satan had the city courted,
  And to marry they agreed.
When the nuptials celebrated,
  They were rudely *charivaried*
Marched a brigade, all red shirted,
  General Booth in chief command,
Proudly o'er them banners flaunted,
  An imposing martial band.

Then they broke the grave-yard silence
  Of the city, lost in dreams.
Drums were beating loud and vig'rous,
  Others thumping tambourines.
All the town awoke in panic.
  Teams took fright and ran away.
Nervous men were seized with frantic,
  And the devil was to pay.

Day and night they kept the racket
  Of the drumming round the town.
Seeing they would never stop it,
  Council met to shut them down.
But the loud noisation army
  Said their mission was from God.
Booth, they thought more wise than Jesus,
  Had supplanted Him as head.

Christ had lacked the special wisdom,
    Money raking to demand
Of the preachers he commissioned,
    As they traveled o'er the land.
Booth preeminence obtaining.
    On his financiering tact,
Now asserts his lordship standing,
    Filling out what Jesus lacked.


Jesus even was so simple
    That He sent His heralds forth
Without drum or tinkling cymbal,
    Nor a tambourine; for-sooth
Taught, if He but be uplifted,
    And His love the people saw,
Through the melting of His Spirit,
    Then to Him all men would draw.


This the Gen'ral thought a failure,
    "Christ alone will never do,
If the world we hope to capture,
    We must march with pomp and show.
A "kingdom not with observation,"
    Will not take in our day;
Ten to one will join religion,
    If we make a fine display."

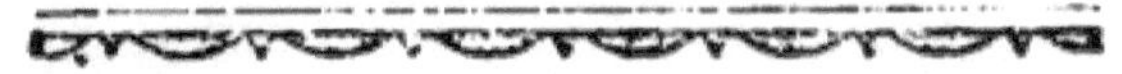

Christ, we read. is "head" and "captain,"
  Of His Church and kingdom pure,
Booth presumed himself commission,
  Into rival office swore;
As it proved a speculation,
  One Moore, thought he'd share the spoil
So they split the clatteration
  In two armies on this soil.


Now they plant their rival forces,
  Fronting each in battle line.
Each to each lift up a "war cry,"
  Bravely smite the tumbourine.
Moore, the traitor, seized the barracks,
  And command in chief assumes.
So they fire on each other,
  With their painted "Quaker guns."


But the safety of Soul-Cripple
  Was endangered by their din.
Drumming, thumping like a rabble
  Nuisance, a shocking sin
'Gainst the sacredness of Sabbath,
  And against all common sense.
All a hollow-drum religion,
  Like the Pharisee's pretense.

So this racketation army
  Was ejected from the town,
And they formed a new edition,
  To the city of renown.
On a dry and desert common,
  Joining on to Quaker street,
Here they serve the god of mammon,
  And their martial glory beat.

Here they drum men out the kingdom
  Of the devil, in their ranks,
Who but glorify the bedlam,
  Lavish on it all their thanks.
Here they spread the banquet table,
  Spend the night in revelry
Mixing Christ in all their babel,
  Hell approved profanity.

Drunkards leave their whiskey guzzling,
  Join the army, loud and brave,
To the pious 'tis so puzzling,
  Drums and tambourines can save.
Time soon proves it no salvation,
  An enthusiastic spell.
Soon the shallow weak sensation
  Leaves the soul enroute for hell

## JOHNSON'S ALL-HAIL EDITION.

While the business of Soul-Cripple
  Made its wanted daily round,
And her crutches selling rapid
  All along her market ground,
And her merchants waxing wealthy,
  By the 'bundance of her trade.
Suddenly there rose a sturdy,
  Who no little trouble made.

All the people of the city
  Were much startled by a sound,
That proceeded from a speaker,
  And re-echoed all around
In the chiefest convocation,
  At the corner of the street,
On a store-box elevation
  Spake the man with zealous heat

So the crippled soul'ans hearkened,
  Horror stricken into mutes;
For that voice so loud and hollow
  Seemed to come up from his boots.
Yea it rattled ; 'gainst the buildings,
  Like an angry threatening row.
So the people came together,
  Wond'ring what was coming now.

And behold ! it was a preacher,
  In a deep and gutt'ral tone,
Crying, "put away your crutches,
  Stand complete in Christ alone.
There's no use of all this hobbling
  On your sinful sectish props,
They're inventions of the devil,
  And their merchants gaudy tops.

"Your divisions are all wicked,
  They engender only strife;
Jesus prayed that His disciples,
  Should be one here in this life.
Not His Word, but your inventions,
  Have begotten party lines.
Therefore burn up all your crutches,
  And repent of all your sins."

This was now an awful message,
  In the ears of Cripple-Soul.
"He's a mover of sedition,
  And a sacriligious fool."
Cried the people in a clamor,
  Neath the smarting of his scourge.
Though much truth was in his hammer,
  Not a coal was in his forge .

But the fierce intrepid scolder
    Was not eas'ly driven out.
So that night he took his corner,
    And resumed his pouring out
Hail and grapeshot on the crutch'ries,
    Quite to break the business up.
So he made the babylon merchants
    Swallow down a bitter cup.


When the loud discourse was over,
    And the benediction bowed,
'Round the speaker there did gather
    Quite an indignati'n crowd.
"Why inveigh against our crutches"
    One and all began to cry,
On them we have leaned for ages
    "And we'll ride them till we die."


Nay, but answered Lyman Johnson—
    For that was the speakers name—
Christ is all we need to lean on.
    But your crutches make you lame.
One then gave this quip rejoinder,
    "Inconsistency you show,
While you smite us with your hammer,
    You your-self on crutches go."

This provoked a burst of cheering.
    When the laughter did subside,
And the stranger had a hearing,
    He vehemently denied.
But rejoined again the other,
    "Do not lie, for it is true,
"Since you left the lap of mother,
    You have rode on crutches too."

"Not a man in all Soul-Cripple
    More than you on crutches ride.
Like your spine your creed is crooked,
    As if satan sat astride.
We have all some kind of crutches,
    And we think it no disgrace,
But the man that keeps his covered
    Best be scarce about this place."

At this Lyman grew more chafy,
    And in loud defence he cried,
"It is false, I have no hobby,
    On no hackneyed props I stride.
Christ is all I want I tell you,
    All your crutches I disdain,
They're a curse to all this city,
    They dishonor Jesus' name."

Then they, pressing round him, rudely
  Raised his sacerdotal gown,
When, behold! to his confusion,
  There the man was hanging down
'Twixt the same old Quaker crutches
  On their market long had stood.
Then great laughter and derison
  Burst from all the multitude.

This exposure drove the pester
  In confusion out the town.
Now there was a Quaker common,
  Held by them and Booth alone ;
North and westward from the city;
  On that bleak and dreary site
He took squatter's right to settle,
  And to carry on the fight.

'Twas a slightly elevation,
  From the great confusion town,
Which advantageous position
  'Nabled him to scatter down
Hail and all annoying missiles
  To molest the devotees.
Riding yet his anti-naggy,
  He'd assail their crutcheries.

Then this Cripple Soul tormenter,
    Struck upon this new device;
Built a great refrigerator,
    That would manufacture ice,
Which, by summer and by winter,
    With an enginery of war,
He threw on the fated city
    All their restless peace to mar.

O what torment and what sorrow
    From that north edition came,
Hail-stones now and ice tomorrow,
    Tripped and stumbled all the lame.
Blood and fire he never mingled,
    All a frigid aspect wore.
So the chilly blasts of Lyman
    Froze their dead religion more.

## RUSSEL'S HOAX-AGE EDITION.

Just what adverse moulding forces
  May have stamped their dire effect
And misshaped the mind of Russel,
  We are not prepared to state.
But it seems that some misfortune
  Sat upon his embryo,
Hence it was, the Holy Bible
  He could not believe was true.

On that Book he sat in judgment,
  Holding it much under par,
By the standard of his wisdom:
  For he thought, 'twere better far,
Had it been confined to heaven,
  And that all must in it dwell;
But, O dear! that dreadful larum
  Of an everlasting hell!

Tho' 'twill do on earth to'prison
  Men who thirst for human blood,
All should freely stalk in Heaven,
  Thief and villain, bad and good.
Since the Word gives faithful warning,
  That the wicked must depart
If they slight complete salvation,
  And so demonize their heart,

 SOUL-CATTLE CITY.

Russel said he would not stand it;
　Unless God revised the Book,
To the wisdom of his ethics
　He'd drop on the skeptic hook.
Since the Scriptures verse his reason,
　And declare there is a hell,
He kicked out of Heaven's traces,
　And became an infidel.


But to be a skeptic merely,
　Did not meet the devil's plan,
That is stale and out of season;
　So, said he, "my faithful man,
You've been bravo 'gainst the Bible,
　And abhorred the thoughts of hell,
But you'll curse the place still louder
　When with us a while you dwell.


"Now I know you love promotion,
　And I've found a place for you,
We've devised, in hell's convention,
　Something altogether new.
Or, at least, we've dressed it over,
　So it cannot help but take,
For the restless hearted sinner
　Wants a cooler for the 'lake.'"

"Once we did a thriving business
    On the universal bate,
But the thunderbolts of heaven
    Knocked it wholly out of date.
So we gave it a new dressing,
    And confessed that hell is right.
But its flames would work redemption,
    And just burn the sinner white.

This was also soon exploded
    And it fell in disrepute;
For in spite of all precaution,
    It showed up in hellish fruit.
So we've now revised the system
    And will make another run
With the same old lie tucked under
    This new garb, "the age to come."

We bestow on you the honor
    To be head of this new plan.
Many soon would jump the offer,
    But we think you are the man.
Therefore publish to all nations
    That a favored age is near,
That will scoop all up to Heaven
    Who have served the devil here.

Need not tell them to be wicked,
    They'll attend to that no doubt,
When you promise them our patent
    Coming age to help them out.
For the works I've planted in them
    Will propel them right along,
Into ev'ry line of sinning
    When the fears of hell are gone.


Mr. Russel bowed politely
    And expressed no small surprise
That, amid his numerous fam'ly,
    He should so conspicuous rise.
"Since," said he, "it's fallen on me
    To be head and patentee
Of this latest shift infernal,
    I'll accept it cheerfully."


So they made a new edition
    To the town of every craft,
'Till too late deferred redemption;
    And for joy the demons laughed
All the sinner's lust unbridled,
    Who believe the soothing lie,
"Now's the time to dance and revel,
    And get pious by and by.

"Your good tidings, Mr. Russel,
  Suits our wishes very well;
For we love to serve the devil,
  But kept back for fears of hell.
The Old Bible has salvation
  Forced upon the people "now,"
But I like your new edition,
  Where the future age will do.

"What's the use to be Religious
  Where it makes the devil rage.
Just keep back, he won't disturb us
  In the Russelsonian age.
And its nice to have his favor,
  In this world where he's at home,
So we'll serve him till he leaves us,
  In the happy age to come.

"The old Bible's far too narrow,
  All its hope must here begin.
So we'll stretch it to another
  Age, to have more time for sin."
On a hellward leaning "Tower,"
  Russel and the devil sit,
While their falsehood loving army's
  Marching onward to the pit.

---

### GOD CALLS HIS PEOPLE OUT OF HER.

While the populace of Cripple
  But corrupted all their way,
God beheld in sovereign pity,
  Some within her prisons lay,
Who were citizens of Zion,
  And were of another heart.
These all heard a voice from heaven,
  Come "my people" thence depart.

Yea, arise, depart "my people,"
  "This is not at all your rest,"
For, alas!   it is polluted,
  T'will thy soul in tophet cast,
And destroy with sore destruction.
  Lest her plagues upon thee fall.
Flee ye out the midst of bab'lon
  And deliver now thy soul.
        Micah-2: 10.   Jer. 51: 6.

Jesus Christ the awful "Breaker"
  Then came up before their face,
To assemble all of Jacob,
  And redeem them by His grace.
So He opened up a passage,
  Through the gateway led them out.
As their King passed on before them,
  All the multitude did shout.
        Micah 2: 12, 13

When the Lord evacuated,
    Left her empty, desolate,
Forth He called the honest hearted,
    He Himself without her gate.
"Come," O come all ye "my people,"
    Or my face no more you'll see,
Hear my voice no more in babel,
    Hasten out and come to me."

               Rev. 18: 4, 23.

Yet within her meshes lingered
    Some who were of "double mind."
Who loved God, but knew not whether
    They could leave all else behind.
Then, with Trumpet loudly sounding,
    Messengers Jehovah sent,
Preaching the Eternal Gospel,
    And commanding all repent.

Robed in spotless white of Heaven,
    Glory shone upon their face.
And their words, an awful hammer,
    Fell like hail-stone on the place.
But there was yet with it mingled
    Flaming fire, and the blood;
These they cast upon the people,
    And extoled the Son of God.

Hail destroyed their false religion,
  While the blood and fire combined,
Cleansed and purged unto perfection,
  All who were of willing mind.
Soon the wood, and hay and stubble,
  Caught on fire all around,
And their fact'ries were in danger
  To be leveled to the ground.

For these heralds spake in power
  Awful burning words of God.
Preaching Christ and full redemption,
  Through His all atoning blood.
Each one had a golden censer,
  Filled with Heaven's holy flame,
Which they cast upon the city,
  In their King's Almighty name.

Then all they who sighed for freedom,
  And abhorred the city's deeds,
Wept for joy to hear the tidings,
  And renounced their dwarfing creeds.
"Long," said they, "we have been waiting
  For the light that shines to-day,
'Tis the truth we have been seeking,
  And we'll tread its golden way.

But now came the days of trouble
  For that city of ill fate;
For the Lord arose to judge her
  In her wicked Sodom state.
So "their faces gathered blackness,
  And "they gnawed their tongues for **pain,**"
For her merchandise was perished,
  Dead and gone her hope of gain.


They were "mad upon their idols,"
  And they strove against the Lord.
Even gnashed upon His servants,
  Just because they preached His **Word.**
Each began at once extoling
  His own hobby very much.
Crying, "Great is our Dianna,
  And all glory to our crutch.


If you burn up all our crutches
  And consume our factories,
You will leave us stripped and wasted;
  For what have we else but these?"
But the holy heralds answered,
  "We are come to do you good,
Even turn you from these idols,
  To the true and living God."

Then spake one for wisdom noted,
    In his town an honored sage,
"That crutches do have God's approval
    Is evinced by hoary age."
"Nay, by fruits we know each system,
    Not by mere antiquity.
Else would sin, the source of factions,
    Yet present the stronger plea."


Then stepped up one Mr. Simple,
    By him-self reputed wise.
In a centumacious wrangle
    Labored loud to 'pologize
For the City's superstition.
    He alleged it indiscreet
For a living man to venture,
    Walking only on two feet.


"For, said he," a pond'rous body
    Can't—a scientific fact—
Rest securely on two proppings,
    Hence our crutch is what we lacked.
If by casting two legs from us,
    We could better get about,
Would we not be yet more supple
    Less two more and do without?"

But they answered, "O ye people,
  "Ye ask counsel at your stocks."
And ye "say your staff declareth."
  So ye lean upon your props.
Erring in your whoredom spirit,
  Egypt is the staff you trust,
And while on it you are leaning,
  It doth in your vitals thrust.
    Hosea 4: 12.  2 Kings 18: 21.   Isa. 36: 6.
"They do "break and rend thy shoulders,"
  Sorely pierce within thy "loins,"
Yet ye make these, your inventions,
  Equal to your flesh and bones,
And as needful as the members
  Of the body, all complete,
God created, standing perfect,
  Unencumbered on its feet.
      Eze. 29: 6, 7.
"Is there life within your crutches?
  Have they veins and coursing blood?
"As if the staff should lift up," bravely
  Yea, "as if it were no wood."
I, the Lord create the body,
  But your props I can't endure,
They insult creative wisdom
  And exalt the creature more.
.Jer. 10: 14, 15.  Isa. 10: 15.  1 Cor. 12: 24, 5 .  Eph. 1:22 22.

"With the God-created body
    You these timbers classify.
Yet you know they're late inventions,
    And your claim for them a lie.
Long before these cripple trappings,
    Was the body Heaven made,
And on it you cast dishonor
    By your counterfeiting trade."

"You've deformed and dwarfed the system,
    By your clumsy headed rails,
And reduced its locomotion,
    To the crawling of the snails.
And you're taxed and drummed to paupers
    To support your cratcheries,
In return you're hanging empty,
    Like a scare-crow in the breeze."

But again rejoined the cripple
    In conceit and bigotry,
"Look out over hill and valley,
    Those green waving fields you see,
Reaching into foreign missions,
    Were all planted, watered tilled
By men leaning on their crutches;
    Would you blast their goodly yield?"

"Nay," replied the herald of Heaven,
    "I'd not blast, but much improve,
And enlarge the fruits of labor.
    Those poor crops can never prove
That your crutch is an advantage:
    They obstruct your arms and **hands,**
As you labor in the vineyard,
    As you hobble o'er the lands.

"If some products have been **gathered,**
    By weak cripples hung on poles,
How much greater were the harvest,
    And the vantage of poor souls,
Had you cast off all encumbrance,
    And like men, erect and strong,
Swiftly gathered in abundance,
    While on props you've moped **along.**

"O ye foolish generation!
    All so well, blind and dumb!
How unfit for distant nations,
    All divided here at home.
You have compassed land and **ocean,**
    See ners ls ostensibly;
But have shamed the very **heathen,**
    Each with rival cratchery."

Then arose another zealot,
  Who avered his crutch the best,
Said he'd not exchange for any
  Other patent on the list.
But the herald answered quickly,
  "God cares not to have you swap,
But flee out this cursed city,
  And give all her business up."


Lo, this caused the man to shudder,
  Filled with horror and amaze.
"O my crutch! my crutch!! my city!
  Rather let the orient blaze,
Never light again my vision;
  Let my tongue forbear to move,
And my hands forget their cunning,
  If my crutch I cease to love!


"Should I cast away my "Method,'
  O what could I lean upon?
I should have to seek another,
  Or soon break and topple dow
So to give up all our crutches
  Would but lead to other kind
And, alas! there're now too many,
  They confuse and craze the mind."

"You would take away our leanings
   And you bid us walk erect,
But this would be unbecoming,
   And a thing we can't expect.
There's none perfect, no none perfect!
   So we can't, *we can't be straight*
Till we quit this life of sinning,
   And we enter Heaven's gate."


Then the angel answered, "Cripples,
   You deny the power of God.
You ignore the great Physician,
   Who hath shed His precious blood,
Thee to save in perfect soundness,
   And respine you by His might,
Put you walking upright, soaring
   Like the eagles sunward flight.


"In His name, the Great Jehovah,
   We must blow this awful blast,
Judgment, ire and full destruction
   On this wicked place is cast.
Therefore all your crutches, idols,
   Gather in a gen'ral heap,
And t' appease the wrath of Heaven
   Burn them, burn them in the street.

"This thy cup that God has given,
  Cup of wormwood and of gall.
Ye must drink it all ye nations,
  "Drink, be drunken, spue and fall."
So they drank the cup of fury,
  And were "moved and mad and fell."
"On their glory shameful spewing,"
  Filled the place with fumes of hell.

Then those fac'tries where the crutches
  Were turned out in great supply,
Soon were wrapped in red destruction;
  And the people raised a cry,
O my crutch'ry! O my crutch'ry!
  Woe is me this evil day.
O my great and noble fact'ry,
  In its ashes soon must lay!

When they saw their pride was burning,
  And their merchandise had fled,
Far at sea her merchants weeping,
  Casting dust upon their head,
Loud bewailed her sudden ruin.
  Saying, "O alas! alas!!
Our great city clothed in purple,
  Lies a burning smoking mass.
            Rev. 18: 15-19.

'Then the angel of Jehovah
  Said to all the holy ones,
"Rejoce Apostles, and ye Heavens
  Over her, as judgment comes."
And they shouted, Alleluia!
  Now is come salvation pure,
And the Kingdom and the glory
  Of our God forever more!

'Then the city was divided:
  All the good and pure and blest
Deeper into God entered,
  And attained His holy rest.
Even 'mid the wild commotion
  Of the city's utter fall,
They resolved to go to Salem.
  And their King was all in all.'

'There all cast away their crutches,
  And began to walk free.
But the children of confusion,
  Though more num'rous, were deject.
For it grieved them sore that many
  Had ignored their wooden gods.
So they gnashed upon the pilgrims,
  Beat them with their stilted hobbs.

And, behold! when Quaker Lyman
 Saw his ice was melting down,
Yet defamed the holy remnant,
 More than all in Cripple Town.
In so much that justice ordered,
 That his name and deeds befit,
This due change should be recorded,
 Namely should be "*Lie-man*" writ.

Now had come the separation
 'Twixt the cripples and the sound,
'Twixt the joyful in salvation,
 And abject on crutches found.
Those set out for true Mount Zion,
 With a bright and joyful hope.
These still linger in the ruins,
 'Mid the dust and ashes grope.

Yea they are so mad confounded,
 And unto their city's fame
Are so blindly yet devoted,
 That amid the very flame,
They do weary them with building
 Structures that the flames consume:
And they close their eyes from seeing
 Babel's judgment and her doom.
   Jer 51 58. Hab.: 2 12, 13.

Fallen! Fallen! is the city,
  And an habitation, drear,
Of each foul and hateful spirit.
  Yea of demons thronging there.
Satyrs dance amid her revels,
  Doleful beasts, and birds unclean,
Goats and imps, and fools and devils,
  Mixing up, combine the scene.

All her priests divine for money,
  Cater to the pride and sin
Of the carnal minded many.
  Whom their net hath taken in.
While the blind lead on the blinded,
  All deceived, deceiving all,
Satan smiles upon the business,
  Death and hell cast on the pall.

Here on her we drop the curtain,
  And shut out the od'ous scene.
O, thou filthy bloody harlot,
  Hell is straitened with thy sin.
Farewell all ye sordid cripples,
  Nay, how can we say farewell,
"Fear, the pit, and snare, upon thee,"
  Must attend thee down to hell.
      Jer. 48. 43.

But adieu. for we must travel
    With the remnant who return,
Fleeing from the fall of babel,
    To the New Jerusalem.
Hark! a noise like many waters!
    'Tis the captive's jubilee.
Like the voice of mighty thunders.
    Hallelujah! we are free!

For, behold! with joyful wonder,
    Just out side the crumbling wall,
Of that hold of craft and plunder,
    There the pilgrims found withal,
First a highway, then a higher,
    "Called the way of holiness."
Here the God of love and power,
    Raised them up to righteousness.
        Isa. 35: 8–10.  Eph. 2: 8.

Here they gained eternal safety,
    From the prowling beasts around.
Lions, vultures, beasts of raven,
    Never shall thereon be found.
But there walk the holy people.
    "And the ransomed of the Lord
Shall return and come to Zion,
    On this highway of His Word.

Now the host in joyful freedom,
  And sweet order move along.
Fill'd with everlasting glory,
  Sounding loud the victor's song.
Nearer, nearer, to Mount Zion!
  Sorrow, sighing flee away.
And the strains of angels harping
  Fall upon them all the day.


More and more the light of Heaven
  Drove the shadows from the day.
Grace and truth were richly given,
  All along the shining way.
Till the pure "beloved City,"
  Burst in grandeur on our sight,
That was hid in captive ages,
  Till the dawn of evening light.


Hallelujah! Glory! Glory!!
  We have found a sweet release
From the straps and yokes of babel,
  From her lords and gruff police.
Free indeed from all confusion!
  Rent the chains of servitude.
Freed, deed! O great salvation!
  Through the blood, the cleansing blood!

Saved from clamor sect and ism.
　From the mold of every creed.
From the curse of strife and schism,
　Dead to all her mammon greed.
We defy the hold of devils,
　And despise her patent rules,
Not a terror in her councils,
　Not a horn upon her bulls.

No Tobiah in the temple,
　To defile the holy fane.
And consume the meat oblations
　That unto the priests pertain.
All his stuff's cast out the chamber,
　And the cleansing is complete.
No more wedding with Sanballat,
　Nor can hell again defeat.
　　　　Neh. 13: 7—12, 23, 24, 28.

All the breaches in salvation,
　Round about Jerusalem,
Are closed up against the nations,
　'Gainst the ites of Babylon.
Moabs, Arabs, Gog and Geshem,
　Egypt, Sodom. Horonites,
Half-bred Ashdods, Sabbath trader
　Canaanites and Ammonites.
　　　　Neh. 6: 1, 2. 13: 10, 23, 24.

So the saints are free forever,
  From the fear of beast control.
To the Kings beyond the river
  Pay no tribute, custom toll.
Free from foreign intervention,
  Circuit tax and revenue,
From Sanballat's sect convention
  In the valley of "Ono."

Free from conf'rence machinations,
  From committee's round of trash.
From preambles, and discussions,
  From the speaker's carnal lash.
Free from making, and revising,
  Laws for Babel's stupid god.
Free from voting, wire-pulling,
  "All a pompous empty fraud."

Priest credentials—a deception
  Only needed by the quack,
Void of Holy Spirit unction,
  Trusting in a musty stack
Of old sermons garb'ed and stolen—
  And Soul-Cripple lesson leaves,
All were bound and left consuming,
  With her thorn and brier sheaves.
Nahum 1. 10.

Not a stone for a foundation,
  Nor to lay a corner down,
Did the ransomed carry with them,
  From old fallen Cripple town.
For their "city hath foundations,"
  And her builder God alone,
Pure as Heaven, whence descended,
  And returning to His throne.

But who is this Holy City,
  As the moon so bright and fair,
Looking forth in all the glory
  Of the morning sun so clear?
Ah! she is the Bride of Jesus,
  His own Church, arrayed in white.
Lo! His beauty is upon her,
  And Himself her crystal light.
       Cant. 6: 10.   Rev. 21.

God is in her, hallelujah!
  And she never shall be moved!
Jesus Christ is her foundation,
  And her righteousness, approved.
All her law is love; and freedom
  Is her balmy atmosphere.
Far more sweet and blest than Eden,
  Is her walk with Jesus here.

All her music is Celestial,
    Sang by angels round the throne,
And then wafted by the Spirit
    To this border-land of home.
All the ransomed sing together,
    In angelic harmony,
By salvation made a unit,
    As in Heaven all agree.


Not a spirit of dissension,
    Nor discordant voice we hear.
For no alien ever entered,
    Nor can ever enter here.
Christ the door, and His salvation
    Is the way to enter in.
And through Him there's no admission,
    Without leaving every sin.


Jesus is our Head and Ruler,
    And His Word our only guide.
And His gentle Spirit leader.
    Is our peace, a constant tide,
Flowing in our tranquil bosom,
    Where is reared the mystic throne
Of the King of peace Eternal,
    Where He dwells and reigns alone.

O the glorious hope of Zion!
  O the riches of her grace!
Ever happy are the people
  Who abide in such a place.
God is over all in Glory,
  And is through them great and small,
And He's in them by His Spirit,
  Jesus! Jesus!! All in all!

# MISCELLANEOUS POEMS.

## TO THE ALIEN.

THREE years have fled since billows wild,
    Wrecked our domestic bark,
And chilled your love for husband, child,
    Mid waters cold and dark.

How wonderful the mystery!
    Astonished, men exclaim,
That hearts so knit in unity,
    Could ever part in twain.

But "some of them that understand—
    In Daniel we are told———11: 35.
Shall fall, alas! in time of end,
    Though white and tried as gold.

Thus wisdom speaks in thunder tones,
  O earth behold His signs!
The end is nigh, the Savior comes,
  How perilous the times!


Our precious boy, so sweet and pure,
  Has lost a mother's love :
His little heart could well endure,
  Were she but gone above.


One mother only nature gives,
  To every child of earth :
But others now supply the place,
  Of her that gave him birth.


O happy day if ever grace,
  Shall melt that heart of thine!
That son may see within thy face,
  A mother's love, Divine.


We suffered some adversities,
  A portion all must find,
When compassed round by devotees,
  Whose creeds we'd left behind

When pressing to the harvest field,
   Of everlasting truth.
And just before the golden yield,
   Alas! you turned aloof.


O how I wish that you could share
   In these ecstatic days:
Enjoy the light of God so pure,
   And help to sing His praise.


My soul had longed for more of God,
   More glory in the cross;
But never dreamed that it must come
   Through such a bitter loss.


I cannot chide His providence,
   But count it all the best;
For in each storm of violence
   I sink to sweeter rest.


'Tis good to learn in furnace flame
   What Christ the Lord can do:
O bless,         thy name!
   He gently leads me through.

'Twas not a rival filled thine eyes,
    With colored fancies rare;
But satan came in deep disguise,
    And wrought the dread affair.


Thus came the fiend in Eden fair,
    The woman's heart to win:
With charming words of wisdom rare,
    He plunged the world in sin.


And so betrayed Delilah, **to**
    The Philistines of old,
Her husband;   when yet feigning true,
    His secret did unfold.


Again in hell the council sat,
    Renewed the cursed plan,
That Adam saw, and Samson met,
    To overthrow the man.


And instrument adroitly used,
    A plot infernal, black,
To quench the burning present truth,
    And turn deliv'rance back.

Loud rang a shout of babel joy,
  Supposing Truth had died:
But forth she came, without alloy,
  The better, being tried.


We still are joined in Eden's bond,
  Of matrimony true:
While life endures yet indissolved,
  It binds my heart to you.


No court of man, or satan's power
  Can disannul the tie:
Though spirits rent, in evil hour,
  "One flesh," are you and I.


No face so fair, no heart so warm,
  Upon this verdant sol,
Shall alienate with rival charm
  The wife received of God.


So I will walk with God alone,
  And bless His holy name,
Till He shall bring the alien home
  To dwell in love again.

In vision of the night I saw—
    And woke to joyful praise—
True nature reimprint her law.
    That ruled thy former days.


From nature's pure affections **then**
    Grace lead to love Divine.
Then Heaven's bliss alone can **bound**
    Our mutual joy, sublime.


God grant that this may real **prove**
    Through coming years of time.
And in His shining courts above,
    An endless crown be thine.


The hand of God alone can **take**
    The broken chords of love.
And knit them in a union, sweet
    As love's pure reign above.


Here I will close my present rhyme,
    But ever pray for you.
That God may give you back again,
    The heart of woman true.

Then touched by sweet seraphic strains,
　　With all the Heav'nly throng
I'll shout aloud my Savior's praise.
　　And sing another song.

# TO MY DEAR SIDNEY

THE heart that feels a father's love,
    And swells with love's return,
Will kindly bear this overflow,
    Toward my only son.

Yes, Sidney's love so blent with **mine**,
    A poem shall employ;
A token left to coming time,
    That father loved his boy.

One gent'e vine, thy tendrils sweet,
    Around my soul entwine.
A comfort left in sorrows deep,
    One heart to beat with mine.

Thy life has dawned in peril's day,
   Mid wars that Heaven shake;
Thy summers five, eventful, they
   Like surges o'er thee break.


Thy little soul has felt the shock,
   Of burning babel's fall;
When hell recoiled in fury black,
   And stood in dread appall.


But wreaking out his vengeance now,
   Like ocean's terror dark;
Hell's monster came athwart the bow
   Of our domestic bark.


Thy guardian angel wept to see
   This brunt of fury sweep
The girdings of maternity
   From underneath thy feet.


But pity still her garlands weave
   Around thy gentle brow;
And angels on thee softly breathe
   Their benedictions now.

They soothe and bless thy manly heart,
  And wipe away thy tears.
So tempered to thy bitter lot,
  The bitter sweet appears.


An exile now is each to each;
  As banished far at sea.
A martyr on his island beach,
  I daily think of thee.


And stronger love has seldom spanned
  The mocking billows, wild,
Than are the chords that ever bind
  To my beloved child.


Though sundered not by angry main,
  Compelled from thine embrace;
We flee abroad in Jesus' name,
  To publish Heaven's grace.


Thy little heart cannot divine,
  Why pappa stays away.
But coming years will tell—if thine—
  The great necessity.

When sickness crushed thy little form,
  I knew my boy was ill;
I heard thee in my visions call,
  But duty kept me still.


A trial deep, to feel thy pain,
  And yet debarred from thee,
To show that sinners lost, were in
  A greater misery.


O may this lesson speak to thee,
  When father's work is done;
And highest may thy glory be,
  A soul for God is won.


And now my son, attentive hear,
  My benediction prayer,
And ever tune thy heart and ear,
  To Heaven's music, rare.


For ere the light of day had shone,
  In thy unfolding eyes;
We gave thee up to God alone,
  A living sacrifice.

And oft repeated wnen a babe,
    To God our child was giv'n;
And Jesus heard the vow we made,
    And wrote it down in Heav'n.


So like a little Samuel, you
    Must answer, "Here am I."
Give all your heart to Jesus too,
    For Him to live and die.


Like Samuel, serve the living God,
    His temple be thy home,
In love obey His holy Word:
    Thy gentle heart His throne.


The Lord is good, my darling boy,
    He touched thy body well, .
And He will bless thee ever more,
    If in His love you dwell.


A new edition may you be,
    Of father's love and zeal,
But enlarged so wondrously;
    That earth thy tread may feel.

# NEW YEARS GREETING.

January 1st, 1890.

———

ANOTHER year has come and **gone**.
So swiftly flows unceasing time.
Forever on and on and on,
With sorrow's groan and merry chime
Commingled in its surging tide.
Time bears along upon its flood
Poor human wrecks, by sin destroyed.
Yet o'er its stream the hand of God
Still bends His bow of hope Divine,
Its hues of love in beauty shine.

Another year of hope and fear
Has swept around its dial plate,
And with it thousands disappear
To higher bliss or awful fate.
God grant to us who yet survive
A heart of fervent gratitude,
And grace that we may wholly live
To glorify the Source of Good.
Then should this be our final year
We'll sink to rest without a fear.

Another year hath brought its store,
  In rich profusion at our feet,
That we should heart and soul adore
  Our Maker's love so broad and deep.
And have you cast your bread upon
  The waters of the passing year,
In hope that what your hands have done,
  Will in much future good appear?
    Then as thy faith so shall it be,
    In coming days thine eyes shall see.

Another year, how was it spent?
  Leaf back its record now and see.
Have from thy life such virtues went,
  That, blessing others, back on thee
Rebounded in a rich reward?
  Or hath the year rolled o'er thy head,
With no oblation to its Lord?
    Then thy own soul thou hast not fed,
      And Christ the Judge will say to thee
      From men withheld, thou hast from me.

Another year! How many more
  Will pass till all the fleeting train
Shall disappear upon the shore
  Of retrospection's endless plain?
Behold the past with signals new,

Has rushed along before our eyes,
Presaging that but very few
　Shall follow 'till, in dread surprise,
　　This world shall see the woeful end,
　　.And all the sons of God ascend

Another year of solemn space
　Leaps forth from vast futurety,
And, winter-girded, starts his race
　Back into past eternity.
Old time once strictly measured off,
　And wrapped around this earthen ball—
For Heaven's plan just long enough—
　Unwinding fast will soon be all.
　　As earth revolves each day and year,
　　The end of time is drawing near.

Another year begins to-day,
　What solemn destinies are hid
Within its folds we can't foresee,
　As on its margin ground we tread.
If from its lap some bitter drop,
　O give us grace to make it sweet.
And bless the hand that holds the cup,
　And makes all things together meet,
　　For good to them who love His name,
　　And move upon His holy plane.

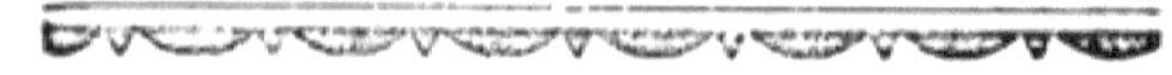

Another year; and with it comes
    A call for valiant hearted men.
All panoplied in Heav'nly arms,
    The tide of sin and hell to stem.
Devoted hearts to God and truth,
    Who dare unsheath and use the sword
Of sin-destroying love, forsooth.
        Win back the humble to the Lord,
            And show through grace and cleansing blood
            How saints made perfect walk with God.

Another year, and who will be
    A hero on its heaving breast?
Fill all its moments as they flee
    With deeds in sacred virtue blest;
And so rear up a monument,
    More lasting than the pyramids?
Yea than the starry firmament.
        True wisdom always highest bids,
            For trophies of immortal good,
            That age-unending honor God.

Another year has now set in!
    O who will take it by the hand,
A new and upward race begin,
    And leave your folly all behind?
How many years you've thrown away,

Spent careless "as a tale that's told."
Awake to life's great end to-day,
And turn thy remnant days to gold.
O be a victor in the strife,
And win a starry crown of life.

# A New Years Greeting.

## 1887

TIME, bearing all to endless fate,
    Has brought again the New Year's chime
And entered on her dial-plate,
    Another year of passing time.


The old, with snowy crest came in,
    And bound the earth in icy pall;
Till came the sweet and welcome spring,
    With nature's resurrection call.


The streams released from winter's chains,
    Now sparkle as they roll along,
And universal nature sings,
    Her praise to God in merry song.

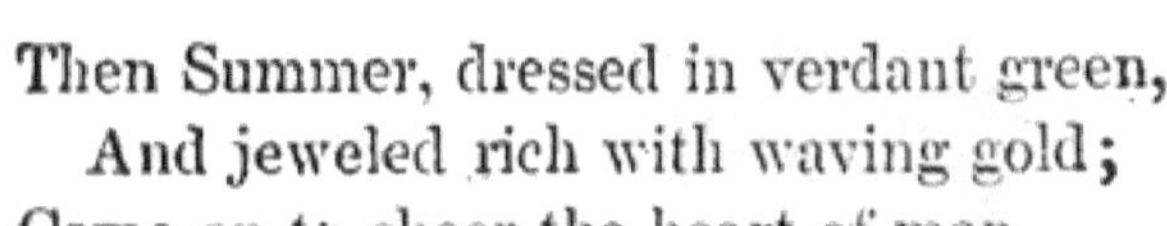

Then Summer, dressed in verdant green,
    And jeweled rich with waving gold;
Came on to cheer the heart of man
    With Heaven's blessings, manifold.


Then Autumn bears its fruitage home,
    In rich and varied bountiness.
O earth behold, and grateful own,
    God's kind and blessed providence!


But greater far the glorious yield,
    Of Heaven's pure and saving Word,
Through all the Gospel Harvest field,
    Some precious souls have found the **Lord.**


O praise the Lord! for one more year,
    Of Father's wondrous keeping power.
How sweet to walk with Jesus here,
    Filled with the peace of God each **hour.**


Like the majestic river's flow,
    Time ever bears our life away;
May all our moments here below,
    Adorn our crown in endless day.

With uplift hand, on sea and shore,
　　That awful Angel will appear,
And swear that time shall be no more,
　　And this may be the very year.

# ❖ LINES, ❖



ANOTHER year of heaven's care,
Another year of blessings rare,
  Have fled, and shall return no more,
  Save all its record, gone before.


In all the voyage years I've passed,
None rocked with billows like the last,
  Against my soul all hell engaged,
  But Jesus calmed each storm that raged.


Each surging wave o' satan's ire,
Each furnace flame of testing fire,
  Has proved a blessing in disguise,
  And helped my soul in God to rise.

Though tender chords have snapped in twain,
Each bitter loss has proved a gain.
O wondrous grace! O love Divine!
That sweetens all our years of time!


The years may come, the years may go.
And with them bear this life below.
My last shall end in heaven's day,
Where all our tears are wiped away.

# ETERNITY.

—

UR inward feelings testify,
With Revelation from on high,
That in this tenement of clay
Dwells something that must live for aye.
   That on this brief expiring breath,
   Which metes our course from birth to death
Hang matters of infinite weight ;
Yea, even our eternal fate.
That bliss or woe in worlds unknown,
Must take their choice from this alone.
Life's game must win a crown of light,
Or barter all to endless night.

   O awful, vast Eternity !
Where comes no change of destiny
Save that progression ever more,—
Through which the soul must higher soar,
And greater bliss and glory know,
Or progress down to deeper woe—

'Which is a law in every soul.
'Worlds and suns may cease to roll,
All the stars that tread the sky,
'May complete their course and die,
But ne'er shalt thou fill up thy age.
And I, somewhere upon thy stage,
Must move along upon the line
My will elected here in time.


What we have sown in life's career,
With all its fruits, will yet appear.
And reap we must, although the yield
Be death itself, the cursed field
Of thorns and tares we can't disown,
Before the Judge upon the Throne.
If to good or bad our sowing tend,
The harvest ne'er shall have an end.
Though pain and grief be all the crop,
And black despair the bitter cup,
When once the bounds of time are past,
The doom is sealed, the die is cast.


O Lord help me to count the cost
Of time,—a single moment,—lost.
A stitch in life's forever dropped,

An opportunity has slipped,
And empty gone into the past,
Nor on one bosom even cast
One gentle sweet beatitude.
O then engage my time dear God!
Give light and wisdom to reveal
Thy will, and grace my heart to seal,
All sacred unto thee alone;
That I may witness at thy throne,
To all assembled worlds above,
The wonders of redeeming love.

# NATURE'S DEVOTION.

————

WE rose this Christian Sabbath morn
   And bowed the knee to Heaven's throne
And worshiped Him whose love had won,
   And changed this heart that once was
      stone.
His goodness passed before our eyes,
   And moved a flood of gratitude.
We wept, o'ercome by great surprise,
   That human hearts irreverence God.

Then we arose drew up the blind,
   And welcomed in the morning rays.
And looking forth far o'er the land
   Love beamed in all that met our gaze.
Lo! God beneath His feet had spread
   A carpet new and soft and white.
So pure! O God! can men here tread,
   And yet be filthy in thy sight?

Ye earthly forms! can ye deserve,
    Or claim your awful Maker's care
If o'er this snowy fleece ye drive.
    Or tread upon its bosom fair,
And catch no sermon from its flakes
    Reproving all thy sins below
The clouds, where God thy Maker makes,
    And scatters down the lovely snow?

Each flake in sparkling purity,
    Descending from above,
As God's adoring messenger.
    Brings silent whispers of His love.
All wove together sweetly form
    A glittering robe of crystal bright;
To show how grace our souls adorn
    In Heaven's garb of spotless white.

Thus nature hath a heart to praise
    The one that gave her voice.
The Moon by night, the Orient Haze.
    And all the stars rejoice.
They seem to glow in ecstacy,
    As if their myriad twinkling eyes
The glorious throne of Heaven see
    High up beyond their vaulted skies.

The ocean sends to heav'n her spray,
   Heaves her majestic bosom high,
And sings her swelling awful lay,
   Or softens to a vesper sigh.
Mirrors the host of heaven deep
   In her Creator's loving hand.
Her rushing billows ever keep
   The boundry fixed by God's command.

The rivers and the little rills
   Sing sweet their praises all along.
While forests and the lofty hills
   In echo, join the happy song.
The restless winds chant through the trees
   The birds are full of fervent praise,
With finer tones the humming bees
   Chime in the universal lays.

The clouds arise like wings of prayer,
   In grateful worship drop their tears.
The fields their varied fruitage bear
   To God, whose goodness crowns the years.
The dew-drops sparkle in the smile
   Of morn, and flowers freely pour
Their fragrant incense from each cell.
   To Him all nature doth adore.

Yes nature seems to be attuned
  To celebrate her Maker's praise.
Man, one exception, hath presumed
  Irreverently to spend his days.
While nature sings in harmony,
  And blesses Heaven's sacred plan,
All things in Heav'n and earth, and sea
  Must shame the prayerless heart of man.

# THE PURE BRIDE RESTORED.

THERE came a time when the angels wept
  And the heavens sighed with pain :
The throne of white wore a sable hue;
  For the Lord afresh was slain.
'Twas when, alas! to the crafty world,
  Turned the virgin Church aside,
And wedlock broke with the Son of God,
  By whom washed, a spotless Bride

Away from God to sects of the world
  Then forth to the dance and feast,
All decked in pride, an apostate vile,
  Far and wide her sin increased.
No more was she the bride of the Lord,
  Though she wore His name, Divine.
By the means of which she hath deceived,
  All the nations with her wine.

Repent, O captive! again return,
  To the Husband of thy youth:
Or feel the woes of a jealous God,
  With a flaming sword of truth,
Smite down His foes, and redeem His Church,
  From the rivals of His Son.
O awful day of His burning wrath!
  Through the earth His judgments run.


His angels fly in the midst of Heav'n,
  With a startling fierce command,
"Fear God.   To Him be thy worship given.
  For His judgments are at hand."
"His mighty ones," all the "sanctified,"
  "For His anger He hath called."
The pure alone can the day abide,
  While the wicked flee, appalled.


All heaven is moved, and the earth is riven
  By the burning of God's ire.
The dragon's host from the Church is driven,
  Neath the hail-storm, blood and fire.
Again appears the Bride of the Lord.
  Pure and spotless through His blood:
A loud voice shouts, "salvation is come,
  And the kingdom of our God."

# LINES,



TAKE now this volume true,
   My child, and let its glow
Light all thy pathway through,
   Up in its counsel grow.

Dear Son this Book revere,
   Its truth thy heart instore,
So peace shall crown thee here,
   And life forever more.

Its leaves with food abound
   For youth and coming years,
In every grief is found
   Some word to dry thy tears.

It tells thee how to spend
   Thy life so pure and good,
That angels o'er thee bend,
   And lead thee home to God.

# GRATEFUL REMEMBRANCE.

WHILE birth-day presents gladden
    The object of our love
There should a warm affection
    Toward another move.

What could more honor justice,
    Requite maternal throes,
Than on our darling's birth-day,
    We drop a fragrant rose
Upon his mother's bosom,
    The instrument divine,
Through whom that gift of Heaven
    Doth sweetly round us twine.

So on this natal morning,
  While from our bosoms flow,
Love-tokens on our darling,
  'Tis meet that we bestow
Some signal of affection
  Where long forgotten pain,
Adorned our habitation,
  With gem of richest gain.

God bless dear Sidney's mother!
  Thank Heaven for this day!
That calls upon a father,
  His debt of love to day.

A debt all means surpassing,
  A claim we ne'er can lift,
So with our greatful blessing,
  Accept this simple gift.

# JAMES AND THERESA.

---

TWO hands on earth are joined,
   Two hearts by Heaven's flame
Into one jewel coined,
   Are now no longer twain.

A thousand miles apart,
   Two streams of life arose;
Each flowing toward a point,
   Now meet in love's repose.

The hand of providence
   Marked out each channel well,
Approaching east and west,
   Till twain one current swell.

Two tributaries meet,
   And gently coalesce,
Both lost in one complete;
   May God this union bless!

Great peace forever flow.
   Within this channel deep,
And on its mirror show
   Love's angels pure and sweet.

Along your verdant banks
   May flowers ever bloom.
And all your life be thanks,
   An endless honey-moon.

The waters rippling move
   Pour music in your ears,
And may the song be love,
   All through your happy years.

May kindness be your star,
   And hope stand high and clear,
And not one fam'ly jar
   Wring out a bitter tear.

Dear James and Theresa now
   We wish you joy indeed :
Kind Heaven bless your vow,
   And all your journey speed.


O may your wedded life
   A tree of virtue prove :
A holy man and wife,
   Will merit Heaven's love.


O let no selfish aim
   Intrude upon your bliss.
That life is only gain,
   That seek all men to bless.

# BERT AND DELLIE.

---

E bless the providence Divine.
    That placed, so warm and true,
Dear Nellie's heart and hand in thine
    Dear Bert, to comfort you.


God bless the pure and gentle bride.
    With Heaven's richest grace!
O Jesus in her heart confide
    Thy everlasting peace.


The hand of God still closer knit,
    The twain in blissful one.
And on their brow a miter set---
    Love's bright and jeweled crown.---

God bless the pair in wedlock sweet
   With long and happy years,
Let angels oft their dwelling greet,
   And drive away their cares.


May Heaven crown this golden bond,
   With blessings rich and rare;
And Kindness weave her tendrils round
   Their paradise so fair.

# CELIA AND RHODA.

---

CELIA and Rhoda, sisters both,
Of the Heavenly Spirit's birth,
Esteemed in heaven of boundless worth!

All consecrated to their God,
Made white as snow in Jesus' blood,
Are very busy for the Lord.

Endued with wisdom very rare,
In office, kitchen, here and there—
Their ready hands are every where—

With unperplexed, instinctive skill,
Frame little birds, their, domicile,
So these, their varied duties fill.

As gentle as the dews of Heav'n,
As silent as the mystic leav'n,
They to their daily work are giv'n.


All hushed but time's slow, measured tick,
And preaching type's more rapid click,
As dropping fast within the stick.


Their fingers fly all o'er the case,
With the musician's utmost grace,
And keep with quickest time apace.


Yea, even quite outspeeding time,
Swift as by magic wheel in line
The type, their telling words combine


Soon line on line to columns grow,
Then round the world their voices go,
And set ten thousand hearts aglow.


From east to west, from sea to sea,
Their labors set poor captives free,
And raise the shout of victory.

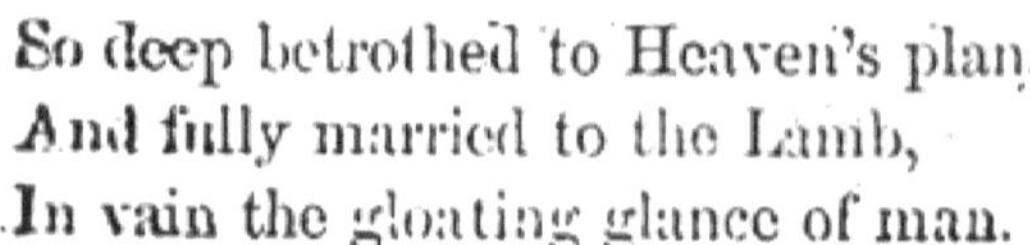

So deep betrothed to Heaven's plan,
And fully married to the Lamb,
In vain the gloating glance of man.


Denying earth's fantastic lure,
Their life a benediction pure.
Their starry crowns in Heav'n are sure.

# A NATION IN CRAPE.

THE world is all in mourning bathed.
  For a nation's Chief* has died.
Him all due tribute we would give
  But all glory th' Crucified.

  Why this pompous cortege and show
    O'er a lifeless bit of clay,
While in this world of sin and woe.
    Christ is crucified each day?

And why all this sombre and gloom,
  For one man, said to be saved,
While throngs, lost, are going to doom,
  Twice dead in sin and depraved.

                    * Garfield.

Eight, ten or twenty miles or more
　　Of crape our city o'er spread,
But do not cover half the doors—
　　Charnels of the LIVING DEAD.


O'er vile saloons, and devil's dens,
　　Sable trappings too appear;
Suggesting death who sways within,
　　Legal murder all the year.


The Nation's blood is all inflamed
　　At the felon's wicked crime;
But think not of our noble slain,
　　By the curse of beer and wine.


If one WITHOUT A LICENSE kill,
　　His death must the crime retrieve;
But poison venders may at will,
　　Glutton hell, and earth bereave.


Oh Nation! then repent thy sin,
　　Lest greater strokes God may send;
Cease to empower agents to kill
　　Those we are bound to defend.

Peace, peace now to the honored dead,
  Grace be to the friends behind ;
The blood the dear assassined shed
  All the Nation's heart shall bind.


But the demise more fruitful still,
  Is soul autopsy, by the Word :
To die to sin, and lie in state,
  Filled with all the life of God.

# OUR FOREMAN.

THERE'S Brother John, for common Bert,
   So faithful at his post—
His pen in motion, quite expert,
   His shout a thund'ring host.

At keeping book and paying bills—
   Oft asking God for means—
He keeps the business moving well,
   In spite of hellish fiends.

Though often tried by wicked pow'rs,
   With sore temptation pressed;
Yet trusting God each testing hour,
   He seems to come out best.

Around his head a daily throng—
    Like swarms of little bees—
His num'rous duties thickly come,
    For hands, and feet, and knees.

Like doves returning to their home,
    From the four winds of Heav'n,
The daily flock of letters come,
    And each attention giv'n.

The form, the press, and engine too,
    His lengthy arms control,
May Jesus bless his labors true,
    And glory crown his soul.

ON THE MARRIAGE OF A MR. HOPE.

IT appeared that Mr. Hope,
Entertained the pleasing hope,
That some hopeless one among the fair,
Was seeking hope from life's despair,
And was pleased with Hope to share,
The cheerful name of Hope to wear.
   And so good Hope went smiling round,
Till the object of his hope was found,
Then sitting by the fair one's side,
Hope beamed with prospects of a bride
The question asked, the prompt decision
Turned hopeful's Hope to full fruition.
And so it happened very soon,
The *beau of hope* became a groom.
Then hopeless changed to hope by name,
And two Hopes but one Hope became.
Their bark now launched on the stream of hope,
May all the blessings hope bespoke,
Their voyage crown along the way
Of Hope's unclouded blissful day.
And may their happy little bark afford,
A lively crew of *sunny Hopes* aboard;
And when to anchor in the harbor driven,
May all their hopes be realized in Heaven.

# ✦ LINES, ✦



**AT THE CLOSE OF AN ARTICLE REPROVING SOME SECTISH**

IDOLATRY.

YOUR craft best thrives
Where virtue dies,
By festives nude,
And frolics lewd.
By games of chance,
And pious (?) dance,
Obtaining pelf,
By lies and stealth
By jockey joles,
And sale of souls.
By taking in
The secret sin,
Your sect may swell,
And prosper well;
And keep apace
In Babel's race,
Of ri–val–ry,
And jeal–ous–y.
Till lightnings flash
The coming crash,
Of Heaven's ire,
"In flaming fire,"
And ruin smite,
The works of n'ght.
And hell possess
Your "Churchliness."

# AUTOGRAPHS

TO SAMUEL AND AMANDA.

MAY your lives flow on together
  Like two streamlets merged in one
Singing, sparkling, bright forever,
  In the light of Heaven's Sun.
God its source, and richly blessing,
  Whereso e'er its channel be,
Twice ten thousand hearts refreshing,
  Each to gem a crown for thee.

Dear child of grace ! strong ties attract thy soul above,
  So let thy heart, by love Divine, be ever sealed,
And all thy life a rich reward and blessing prove,
  When in His glory Christ shall be revealed.

May all your life contribute to
   The store of human bliss,
And doing good rebound on you.
   The joys of righteousness!

As on these leaves of amber white
   We trace some lines of love,
So life's a volume dark or bright,
   All written down above.

So let thy heart and will agree
   To furnish Heaven's roll,
With only thoughts of purity
   That will reward thy soul.

Life is a volume we must fill,
   Be it large or small;
For there are traced each act we will,
   If good or bad they fall.

Thy book of life is just begun,
   Each moment adds a line.
In virtue may the record run,
   And crown thy end of time.

Each day turns o'er another page,
　'Till life's brief sketch is done.
May all be valiant on this stage,
　'Till God will say, "come home."

Give all your youth, and coming days
To God in truth, and pious ways,
'Then life will glow, with peace and love
While here below, and homed above.

# THE CRUSADES OF HELL,

## PART I.

### THE FALL OF MAN.

THE stars that sang creation's birth,
  When wisdom laid her corner-stone,
And all the sons of God, for joy,
  That shouted loud from Heaven's **dome,**
Beheld with solemn painful look,
  The brunt of satan's deep devise.
When hell, and sin this planet shook.
  And moved it out of paradise.

The workmanship of God so pure,
  Suburb of Heaven's City fair,
This earth once bloomed an Eden home,
  In gentle Paradistic air.
Her lord was made in image true,
  Of Him, the holy Lord of all.
Oft heard the happy family,
  The steps of God, their Father's call.

But struck by sin's infernal blast,
   A million miles now intervene,
Between this world, in ruin lost.
   And it's primordial lofty scene.
Distorted, it's polarity,
   A horoscope, conceived in sin,
Earth sank to hell's environment,
   There whirled mid black confusion's din.

All wickedness in every thought,——Gen. 6: 5.
   And bent to sin and vice alone.
Tow'rd God, his Maker indevout,
   To every menial idol prone.
Remorseful now his loss to know,
   Consumed in lust of base desire,
Vile man still plunged in deeper woe;
   Of hell his passions set on fire.

Beholding thus the race corrupt,
   Repented God that man had made.
And after duly warning all,
   Jehovah's wrath no longer staid.
Forth brake the flood, the billows meet,
   Submerging earth—worse 'gulfed in sin—
Like mill-stone cast in ocean deep,
   Save Noah's ark, and those within.

Swept clean the earth her Sabbath's kept,
    No tongue profaned it's Maker's name.
But with the growth of Noah's seed,
    Sin raised its hydra form again.
Then from Mount Sinai's burning top
    God thundered forth a rigid code,
The violence of man to check,
    Till came that "Seed," the Son of God

# THE CRUSADES OF HELL.

## PART II.

### THE BLOODY POLICY OF THE FIRST CRUSADE.

Four hundred years had slowly passed away.
Since dropped the curtain of prophetic day;
Since Mala' closed that bold and faithful line
O seers who thundered burning truth Divine.
Oft rising early, importuning men,
Jehovah spake through prophet's vivid ken.
Now hushed each lip that glowed by Heaven's spark
All men sat waiting, musing in the dark.

But even silence spake in solemn tone,
And darkness brooded hopes of David's throne,
And daily glowed the sacrificial fire,
Where flowed the typic blood of God's Messiah.
There waited Phanuel's daughter night and day,
The Savior's coming earnestly to pray,
'Till witnessed, in the temple Simion's eye,
The consolation promised ere he die.

No sooner dawned the Dayspring's golden age,
Than moved the fiends of hell with livid rage.
Well knowing satan, Heaven's Kingdom is
That mystic stone that would demolish his.
Thus doomed the kingdom devils arrogate,
As came the "blessed only Potentate"
To break in pieces every rival throne,
And reign eternal King of Kings alone.

Hell's fur'ous envy sought, as eager prey,
The tender plant of human hope, to slay.
A kingly heart his jealousy inwrought,
And restless fears his throne should come to naught,
Then vainly filled with diabolic plan,
The murder of the infant Son of Man.
Through Palestine the bloody edict runs,
Inflicting death on Rachel's fondling sons.

At Jordan's stream the bridal servant stood,
And pointed out the blessed Lamb of God.
And, merging from His deep symbolic grave,
The Spirit came, in body shape a dove.
Then summoned in the dreary wilderness,
Long fasting, hunger-smit in deep distress
The Savior met in conflict Heaven's foe,
Repulsing him with honor's stunn'g blow.

Unmoved the Son of God, by satan's wiles,
O'ercoming in the hour of deepest trials;
The fiend recoiled, chagrined at his defeat,
His legions called, in pandimony meet.
To whom discoursed their King, with fallen mein,
Of his reverse, while groanings intervene.
His lords responded, each his plot to show,
Emanuel's Kingdom best to overthrow.

Each harangue stirred the animos of hell,
To hissings, groans, and din of fiendish yell.
Then to infernal counsel cooled again,
All clamored that the Prince of Peace be slain.
To black His name with vilest infamy,
Hell chose to nail Him to the cursed tree.
Meantime let evry lying tongue employ,
His character to tarnish and destroy.

'Twas done, for so had Heaven pre-ordained,
To perfect Him by suff'ring ere He reigned.
So bowed the Son of God His head and died,
The Just, for sinners lost, was crucified.
But death and hell, defeated as before,
Unbared the risen Christ their prison door.
So rose the Prince of Life from death's domain,
To break from man the monster's vassal chain.

"ALL YE INHABI-TANTS OF THE WORLD AND DWELLERS ON THE EARTH, SEE YE, WHEN HE LIFTETH UP AN EN-SIGN ON THE MOUN-TAINS; AND WHEN HE BLOWETH A TRUMPET, HEAR YE." ISA. XVIII.
"FIRST PURE." Then
"VALIANT for the truth."

So trod the wine-press Heaven's lowly Lamb,
And wrought redemption for the race of man.
While sitting neath sin's dark and gloomy night,
There shown on men the dawn of Heaven's light.
And Zion fair, by prophets oft foretold,
Appeared on earth, God's Church of purest gold.
Up to her summit many nations flow,
And in her light their joyful spirits glow.

But will the fiend, earth's usurpation lord,'
Leave, undisturbed, this paradise restored ?
Repelled by Christ the Living Head of all,
Will not his vengeance on the members fall ?
His nature vile, and vicious all his bent,
Shall he forbear ? from hellish deeds dissent ?
Nay, hell is moved to deepest, foulest pit,
And demons vie, in bloody counsel sit.

An insult to the throne of sin and death,
All subjects of the sceptre righteousness.
Fell hatred, murder, and malignity
Are satan's laws : while love is anarchy.
So virtue, deemed by satan's goverment
A crime deserving death or banishment,
Inflamed with burning fury hell's domain,
To torture saints with prison rack and flame!

Nor long perplexed were satan's wily clan,
For instruments to execute his plan.
While a religion, minus love Divine,
The hearts of men with bigotry enshrine,
His ready servants such will ever be:
Their god in danger burns their jealousy,
Which is the devil's richest harvest field;
Its bloody vintage, persecution's yield.

Forth stood the whited sepulchres at hand,
Sin-blinded for their father's fell command.
Their pharisaic garments stained with blood
Of Him they crucified, the Son of God.
To Stephen was the martyr's honor given,
The Jewish stones promoting him to Heav'n.
Him followed many a noble sacrifice,
To wear a purchased crown at martyr's price.

The whipping post, the prison's gloomy cell,
Wild beasts of prey, and chopping blocks as well,
Were utilized to quench the mighty truth,
And kill the worshipers of God forsooth.
When filled the measure of malevolence,—
The Jewish cup of red intolerance—
Brim full, and on them poured by Heaven's ire,
God quenched that nation's persecuting fire.

But brief the respite to the virgin Church.
Meantime hell pried with diligent research,
How to enlarge his enginery to kill,
And greedy thirst for saintly blood to fill.
His gloating eyes to Pagan god's are turned,
There hissing up the smoldring fires that burned
On idol shrines.   Till roused that eagle Rome,
To tear, with vengeful talons mercy's throne.

An Empire, universal, iron strong,
The fiendish foe of man now hisses on.
Mixing idol-bane with fell despotic pow'r,
The infant Church of Jesus to devour.
A thousand martyrs honor Heaven's grace,
Ten thousand enter joyfully their place.
But satan, waxing desperate, yet more
Inventions sought, to fill the land with gore.

The guilct'ne, to sever head and heart,
And quench the light of Heaven they impart.
Hell's inquisition, where fierce demons sit
In human form, but inward from the pit.
Whose bloody-hands extinguish mortal life,
By every instrument of torture rife.
Or terrify, were 't possible, a saint,
The faith of his Redeemer to recant.

But floods of persecution pour in vain!
The rack, and gibbet, and the burning flame.
Yea inquisitions, 'mersed in holy blood,
Can never quench the truth and love of God.
Straight from each scene of honored sacrifice,
There mounted up a soul to Paradise.
And from the ashes of each burning pile,
Up seemed to stand a bold, and num'rous file.

'Till satan, it appears, began to cloy,
At countless millions he must needs destroy,
If by martyrdom he would succeed,
To exterminate the holy seed.
Or rather, satan now began to be,
Perplexed with doubts of his own policy.
Observing that the more he beat the fire,
It spread the more abroad, and flamed the high'r.

Then hell bethought, in deepest quest to know,
Why futile his attempts to overthrow
The pillared temple of the Living God,
And check the onward march of Je us' Word.
Ere long the wily fiend discovered, lo!
That death and suff'ring only served to show
The love and peace that in a Christian shine,
And prove the system Heavenly, Divine.
Then devils groaned to find their deeds at last,
O'er ruled, to serve the cause they thought to blast.

# THE CRUSADES OF HELL.



## PART III.

### FAILURE OF THE 'SECOND CRUSADE.

Then satan, burning with defeat,
  More desperate became.
His legions, summoned at his feet,
  In hellish council came.
Forth rose the great Apolyon chief,
  Mid din of hiss and yell,
And burning fires reef,
  That shook the depths of hell.

Thus spoke the diabolic fiend,
  "Dominions! mighty lords!
Your utmost wisdom all combine,
  In consultation's words.
Some wiser scheme or strategem
  Than bloody martyrdom,
We must devise for future plan,
  One hitherto unknown.

Then Moloch, fiercest power of hell
  Loud spake with utmost ire.
He deeming nothing half so well,
  As slaughter, blood, and fire.
Next Belial, more considerate,
  Maturer counsel sighs,
"That death can ne'er exterminate
  The seed it multiplies."

Next Mammon rose with grave address,
  His counsel forth to gleam.
"Most noble peers! we must confess,
  That 'twere but folly's dream,
To cope with Heaven's lofty Throne.
Until Eternal fate shall yield
  To chance's fickle nod,
We may not hope our sway to wield
  O'er the Almighty God.

And yet our futile war to wage,
  Against the Church of God;
Were to assault His heritage,
  His own select abode.
As well might hope her prestige lend,
  'Gainst the Omnicient Sire,
As crown a war against His Fold,
  His throne of living fire."

Then rose up—next to satan's rank,
   A pillar strong of state—
Beelzebub's atlantean form,
   And gaining audience spake.
"Thrones! powers! proud offspring of Heav'n!
   Grave questions here arise:
How vict'ry to our cause be giv'n?
   What project best devise?

"From persecution's fruitless fire,
   We may as well desist
But who can tell how else conspire,
   This Kingdom to resist?
Athwart my mind there gleams a plan,
   Most noble peers attend!
Let us affect to turn amain,
   This hated cause befriend.

"Instead of war we'll kindness show
   To all believers round.
All hell extol the christian name,
   Good will on earth abound.
Though subjects many we shall lose,
   By bidding them God-speed.
Yet they who go by our consent,
   Will not be saints indeed.

So we will feign to have espoused,
    What we could not destroy;
Our hatred to the truth disguise,
    The pilgrims to decoy,
Down from their high and holy way.
    And by this bait we'll tole
Them into fellowship with us,
    And so corrupt the soul."

All hell broke forth in loud applause
    To hail the good advice.
Then satan rose and second gave,
    Completing the device.
"Much wisdom," saith he, "we have heard,
    But deeper still I see:
More than befriend, we'll join the Church
    And each a member b .

"For if we gain advantage ground,
    Assuming to be friends;
Much more within the Chure 's  ad,
    We shall achieve our ends.
There, to attain each office seat,
    We'll work the wires well,
And gaining rule, we can defeat,
    And cast her down to hell.

"Our nature we will galvanize,
    In penitence appear
Low at the door with weeping eyes,
    And pray admittance there.
Our persecutions we'll repent—
    Because they proved in vain—
We'll seek a place within the Church.
    And help to build the same.


"But dwelling in the Church of light,
    All holy we must feign,
And *don* the saintiy robes of white;
    Still devils we remain.
Though hating all the holy seed,
    We'll play the christian fair;"
For devils prone to black deceit,
    As well as open war.


So hell agreed upon the plan,
    To join the Living Church.
And, satan leading, forth they came,
    The entrance for to search.
Like mourners now the fiendish crew
    Their wickedness deplore.
But shrink amazed as, lo! they view,
    That Jesus is the door.

Then looking up in fear beheld
   "Her walls were great and high,"
Their altitude no fiends ascend,
   Their strength all hell defy.
Then passing round with eager eye,
   A second time, and thrice,
No other ingress could they spy,
   No other door but Christ.

Her bulwarks reach to Heaven's throne,
   God's glory her defense.
Her great foundations deep and strong,
   All frustrate our pretense.
No threshold but th' Eternal Son!
   Can devils enter Him?
Behold His eyes as lightning run,
   Inapproachable by sin.

"That flaming door we can but hate,
   But enter and despoil,
We will, unless eternal fate,
   Our conjurations foil.
So let us search Emanuel's Book,
   Perchance to find a clue,
Or some condition we may brook,
   By which to enter through.

"What mode of entrance has the Church?
    Read now the Book and see.
Tis by a new and second birth,
    What'er that process be.
But who can tell us what this means?
    "Ye must be born again."
To us it very foolish seems,
    Nor can the gods explain.


"Whence came the Church?   From Heaven's
    A golden City fair.                    [throne
Were she produced by human skill.
    We might admittance share.
If only formed on earthly plain.
    Then devils might come in.
Then we'd assume the Christian name,
    And join the social ring.


"What is the Church?   The Body of
    The Son of God Himself.
May devils hope to gain that place,
    By stratagem or stealth?
Each member is a part of Him,
    The fulness of them all;
And like Him must be free from sin,
    Though great, or even small

"What is the Church?   Her elements
    Are love and truth Divine.
With her pure gold of holiness,
    No dross of sin combine.
Within her burns a fire intense.
    From Heaven's furnace—love.
Which flame, upon unrighteousness,
    Far worse than hell would prove.


"If creatures did but organize
    The structure of the Church;
We'd, like a noble pillar rise,
    They'd set us in as such.
But now has God the members set,
    All in their order true ;
He leaving all the sinners out,
    And us poor devils too.


"Or turned but man the Churchly key,
    And passed the seeker in,
We'd knock and pray as loud as he,
    And so admittance win.
But He, the Porter of the sheep,
    Alas ! we know too well,
And worse than all, He, knowing us,
    Would blast us back to hell."

Just then there burst a shout of praise,
  From all the ransomed host,
Their songs like mighty thunders rose,
  Filled with the Holy Ghost.
Then, seized with terror, satan's camp
  From Zion's mountain flit ;
In fear and wild disorder scamp
  Back to their native pit.

Hell sat amazed in horror mute,
  Struck dumb at Zion's sight.
Deject, bewildered at their rout,
  Their prestige smit with blight.
Then gath'ring pluck at last to rise,
  Thus satan, loth, began.
"To join the Church, we thought us wise,
  Now fools, we never can.

"Yet finding out our folly may
  Add some to wisdom's store,
So, by our failure, we to-day
  Know more than heretofore.
Though what we've learned. we wish were not—
  Ill-fated to our scheme—
Yet, knowing hell must be our lot,
  We'll cling to valor's dream."

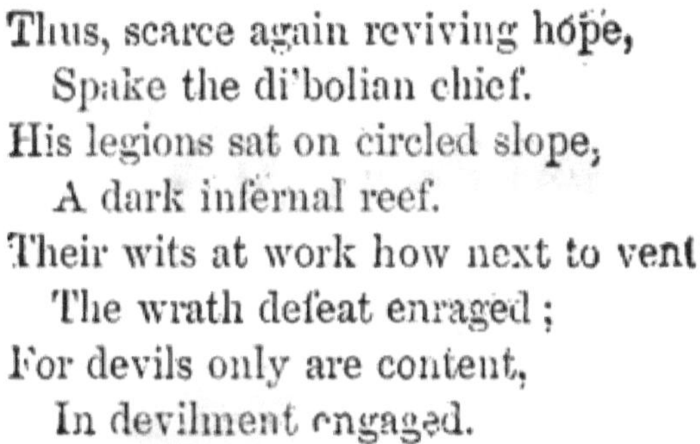

Thus, scarce again reviving hope,
   Spake the di'bolian chief.
His legions sat on circled slope,
   A dark infernal reef.
Their wits at work how next to vent
   The wrath defeat enraged;
For devils only are content,
   In devilment engaged.

# THE CRUSADES OF HELL.

## PART IV.

### SATAN'S THIRD AND LAST CRUSADE.

All hell's infernal ministry
  Was summoned to the task,
Of projecting some new policy,
  And this was struck at last.
The chief of devils rising said,
  "Comrades! since martyrdom
Has failed, likewise our last crusade,
  Let's try this stratagem.

"Since war cannot exterminate,
  Nor can we join the Church,
We'll make to it a counterfeit.
  We'll institute a search
For some aspirant dignities
  Who wear the Christian name,
To draft its creed, to organize,
  And introduce the same.

We'll flatter and insinuate
    A ritualistic zeal,
Assemble councils, grave and great,
    And help to turn the wheel.
We'll whisper in those Bishop's ears,
    And get them fall in line.
To tinker up a human thing,
    A church we all can join.

And if it ever gets exposed,
    We'll get some better men,
To cut and frame as they're disposed,
    And reconstruct again.
And should they get more truth inwove,
    We'll warp in more of sin.
Truth mixed will only more deceive;
    Just so we can get in.

So hell employed the policy
    Of many traps, with bate
Disguised beneath a sacred name.
    Their mischief and their fate.
Read in Chronicles of Cripple-Soul.
    And what that town befell
When all the good, and true and bold,
    Came out the gins of hell.

# FAITH.

---

In this poem the author is conscious of having struck the most vital and fruitful theme that could engage our thoughts. Faith, indeed, is the great all-essential condition of our redemption, and of all our strength, happiness, and usefulness. Were it not that time is pressing us, to issue this work according to announcement we would love to enlarge our labors on this glorious theme.

# FAITH

—

NEED yet an heir of Heaven blush to own
Allegiance to the Universal throne?
Misgive himself in setting to his seal
That God is true, and that His works reveal
That He is love and tender sympathy?
While all His atributes in harmony,
Invite the struggling human heart to rest
From all its fears and cares upon His breast.
In Him the just shall live by faith secure,
The holy Book of Truth, Divinely sure,
The basis of His everlasting trust.
  And yet the skeptic lifts his haughty crest,
And flings this taunt against the Christian's shield,
"Your faith is naught but superstition's yield.
In all the range of human thought around
Hath such a thing as faith no where been found
Save in religion's dark and mystic sphere,
Where manhood yields to superstitious fear.

And only he who chanced to have the gift
Of blind credulity, can ever lift
The vail, and enter faith's domain, obscure:
And that by reason's utter forfeiture.
Tis mental imbecility to act
On propositions not by knowledge backed.
And he's incautiously unwise and lame
Who takes as truth, and ventures on the same,
Before it's demonstrated, proved and known.
Or if not knowledge, then at least the source
Of faith should be an overwhelming force
Of evidence, to so preponderate
The mind, compelling faith's inalternate.
Since faith comes by the gist of evidence,
Where it is clearly in preponderance,
Faith must ensue involuntarily.
But men in gen'ral, with impunity,
Have always set aside the Bible's claim.
Hence its supporting evidence is lame.
Or otherwise all men were forced to yield
Subjection to it, as from God revealed."
   Such paralogy, and deceptive lore,
Some babblers, by false doctrine blind, adore.
But they are sin-born philosophic lies,
Soul bane, in cloak of logical disguise.

# WHAT IS FAITH.

Under this head we will  confine  our song, simply to the faith  of  the  Gospel,  to a few  of the many uses which faith is to the human heart and soul.

# WHAT IS FAITH.

WHAT then is couched within that wondrous word
Which opens all the treasures of the Lord,
Appropriates an endless life of bliss,
Endows the soul, in worlds to come, and this,
With virtue, glory, honor, endless peace
And from all sin and woe its sure release?
Does she, the channel of such special good,
All dfienitions here on earth elude?
Nay, faith does not in superstition grope;
But she's the "substance of the things we hope,"
"The evidence of things we do not see."
O'er earth, and sin, and hell, our victory.
The Faith we sing is no such stupid thing,
That her warm hands of love no trophies bring
The bosom of her friends who give her place.
O blessed is that heart lit by her face!
Faith's not blind, but, blest with genr'ous eyes,
Beholds and chooses out life's highest prize.
Nor deaf.   The music of eternal sphere
Float down with inspiration o'er her ear.

And well she hears the glorious Gospel sound,
Pronouncing all its truth the solid ground.
   She hath feet, hence by faith our soul can walk,
Nor should on stilted feelings try to stalk,
Nor soar on wings of ecstasy around,
Without thy feet of faith upon the ground
Of truth, the sure foundation, broad and high:
Adrift from truth, thou and thy faith must die.
   Faith hath life. By her life the just shall live.
She only hath eternal life to give.
As hath the Father life upon the throne,
So hath He freely given to the Son,
Who to faith exclusively confined
His life, but through her wills it all mankind.
   Faith is not dumb, she hath a mighty voice.
Her music on earth is Heaven's first choice.
Lo! she speaketh!  "Faith speaketh on this wise;
"Say not in thy heart, who'll ascend the skies,
That is to bring Jesus down from the throne.
Or who in the deep for us will go down,
That's to bring up Christ again from the dead.
But these are the words kind faith hath said;
I am nigh thee now—so freely believe—
Yea, in thy mouth and in thy heart, to give
Life, Eternal life, by thy confession,
And thy heart believing to salvation."

Long arms hath faith, and hands omnipotent,
And their might to the humble soul is lent.
Ah! sin hath palsied all the strength, our own.
No hand can we lift unto mercy's throne.
But, saith angel faith, "I'll be arms for thee,
Thy will, and my strong hand shall set thee free.
My arm I will stretch far up to Heaven,
And touch the blood that speaks thy sins forgiven
Take to thy soul my hand, and by it grasp
The gift—Eternal life—and so hold fast
"The profession of thy faith evermore;
And no sin shall henceforth thy life obscure.
My hand hath access to the Book of God,
And I'll write thy name with the "precious blood."
On the fam'ly roll of the Sons of light,"
And I'll hand thee down a robe ever white."

"Now behold by faith's all sweeping vision,
In the center of Love's constellation,
A star of beauty and effulgence shine.
By my hand you may pluck, and call it thine.
Unlike the moon's pale beams that soon must wan,
'Tis an endless Sun in the soul of man.
Its name thy joyful heart and tongue confess,
THE GLORY and "BEAUTY OF HOLINESS."
"Doth not," saith Faith, "thy unmailed breast expose
Thy soul to all the daggers of thy foes?

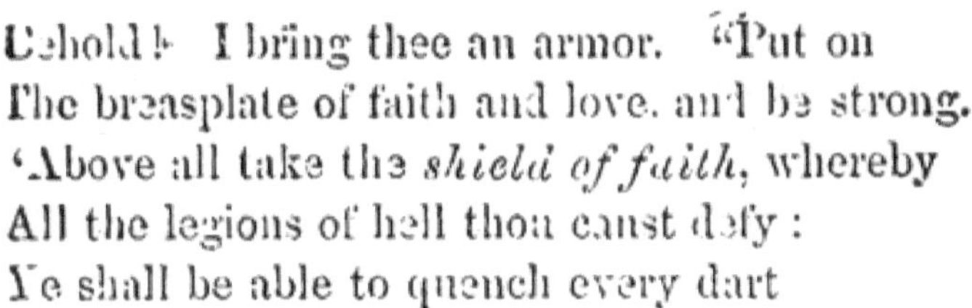

Behold!  I bring thee an armor.  "Put on
The breasplate of faith and love, and be strong.
'Above all take the *shield of faith*, whereby
All the legions of hell thou canst defy :
Ye shall be able to quench every dart
The wicked in wrath may shoot at thy heart.
    I too, faith sang, am the root of thy joy,
A constant source of rest naught can destroy.
Emotional joy may rise and may fall,
Our feelings transported, or feel not at all,
The comforts of hope all brilliant and high,
Or clouds of sombre o'er sweeping our sky :
Every joy of the heart its changes hath,
But the sweet, immutable "*Joy of faith*."
It is based on the Rock of Ages firm,
Which ne'er can take a fluctuating turn.
And as Truth never rises and falls amain,
The faith that is on it must stand the same,
And the joys of that faith for e'er endure,
As the faith itself, and its ground are sure.
    So Faith, to our soul, is our ears and eyes
Our hands and our arms, that reach to the skies,
And pluck from the beautiful tree of life.
Our shield of protection amid the strife.
We believe and therefore we speak the same
So its spirit is testimony's flame.
O precious angel Faith!  Our joy complete !
Ever dwell in our heart, strong, pure and sweet.

# FAITH UNIVERSAL.

ON this line of thought we acknowledge our in leb'e'ne's to a volume of "discourses on the nature of faith," by Wm. H Star. In the main his analysis and definition of faith is very clear and practical.

Some devout reader may take exceptions to our classification of that faith principle which actuates all human exertion, with the faith in God that saves the soul, and unlocks the store house of His blessings. But a careful examination of the matter will satisfy any thinking mind, that the act is philosophically the same, whether it grasps spiritual or earthly objects. True the causes and results of faith in God, differ much from those of faith in earthly projects. In the former, Revelation is the basis of our faith; and, owing to man's spiritual death, the grace of God is essential to unfold the light, and quicken our latent powers of faith. While faith in natural things, is only animated by natural prospects and inducements. In the former instance, faith grasps the power of the Almighty, and a stupendous miracle is wrought; or rather a combination of miracles, by which an entire revolution of our moral being is produced. In the latter, faith but grasps, and wields the mental and physical elements of this world, and reaps temporal benefits. And as God is greater than all the forces of nature, the faith that lays hold on Him, is more exalted in cause and effect, than that which is confined to earthly ambitions; and yet both are the same in kind; being the assent of the mind to a supposed truth, and the act of the will upon the same, through the inducements connected with the proposition in either case. When the apostle said, "All men have not faith," he evidently meant, faith in Christ. But the same Apostle tells us that they "who believe not the truth, but have pleasure in unrighteousness" are also believers. Namely they "believe a lie,"—2 Thess 2; 11, 12.

## FAITH UNIVERSAL.

———

The restless skeptic would argue in vain
That faith's excluded to religious brain.
But we shall prove that they, as do the just
All live by their faith, and maintain some trust.
That all may comprehend just what combine
The elements of faith, we will define
Its sphere of action and simplicity.
And by thus tracing out its province see
Just where and how an act of faith proceeds,
From whence the act springs, and what succeeds.
A proposition demonstrative shown,
Or by experience yet more certain known,
If acted on is no faith act or deed ;
For that which is known doth faith supersede.
Faith, then hath its proper range of action,
Not on truths known by past demonstration
But truths made probable by evidence ;
By a chain of cordial facts, from whence
Conviction rises in the thoughtful mind,
Which, with motives and inducements combined,

Wins assent, and moves the will to act upon.
Then acts of faith these elements embrace,
A proffered truth, to which the mind can trace
Some supporting facts that assurance wake.
Which evidence the heart and judgment take.
To that supposed truth assents the mind,
The will too acting on it, thus inclined
By evidence, but yet by motives more.
  The act of faith thus rightly analyzed,
The fact ensues—though it may thee surprise—
That all voluntary action of our race
To faith, as its fountain, we clearly trace.
While energy moves a living frame,
Or effort of thought in a human brain,
While the arm and hand busy life-work ply,
Until crost on the breast they silent lie,
Yea! while life prolongs its tenuous day,
And our falt'ring steps hold on their way,
Whether strides that press toward the world to come,
Or toils that abound in our temp'ral home,
What we do or say upon life's short path,
All, all we undertake are works of faith.
  Does a farmer know when he plows his field,
That time will bless him with a harvest's yield?
Nay! he plows in hope, and he sows, forsooth,
As an act of faith in a probable truth.

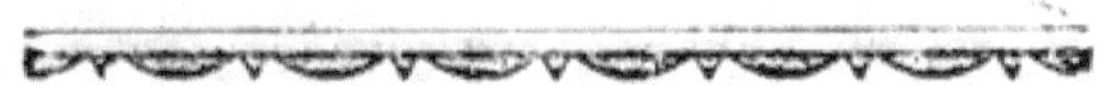

Were the skeptic's logic to assume the throne,
Which denies assent 'till the truth is known,
And will take no step 'till the ground is proved,
Then would the last plow-share the earth have moved;
All farmers cease from their hopeful labor,
And beg or steal from their next door neighbor,
'Till all the store that the earth had produced
While good sense yet reigned, had become exhaust.
And the fields lay waste, with no crops to cheer,
'Till the last man starved on the skeptic's sneer.
  When a blacksmith forges an implement,
See him blow and smite 'till the sparks are sent,
Thick and fast around as the rays of light,
From an old tin lantern in the darkest night.
But what are the terms in his dingy shop?
No, '*pay in advance*," has he posted up.
Nay! he takes the task with a cheerful smile,
And proceeds to pound to drill and file,
Nor wipes off a hint with his honest sweat,
'Till the last lick rings, and the job's complete,
Say, did he know that toil would yield him bread?
No, many a hopeful job he'll ne'er be paid.
So it is by faith from the morn 't'll night,
His brawny arm is nerved to blow and smite.
And even though his dusty books can show
A thousand figures hopeless long ago,

He undertakes each job in all his line,
By faith for cash, or slender faith on time.
　Likewise all carpenters and tinners drive
Their craft by faith, and only faithful thrive.
Shoe-makers, tailors, and machinists too
Their varied lines of work by faith pursue.
And every craft beneath the shining sun,
By faith, more truly than by steam, is run.
E'en toil remunerated in advance,
Where the wages earned runs no dub'ous chance,
These are yet works of faith, as we can show,
Involving points of trust they do not know,
And objects contemplated yet at stake.
Is the blacksmith certain that nail will take
The proper course beneath his rapid lick?
Or turning toward the coffin pierce the quick?
Does the builder know, when he starts a nail,
That the blow he aims surely can-not fail?
And does he trust, or absolutely know
That the nail is strong to receive his blow?
Will it pierce the wood, or to pieces break?
These and other risks he by faith must take.
　When bankers loan upon security,
However safe they think the case to be,
'Tis but a probable truth at best,
Upon which his idolized dust is cast.

So he plays by faith when the best is done,
And appeals to time whether lost or won.
   So the lawyer pleads his client's case,
Staked on the proposition that his race
With rival attorney will fetch up won;
Or that both may drink their bumpers and smile.
O'er the fine grist sacked in the court house mill;
Where their clients were ground, and their green-backs
And they sent home with neither bran or toll. [stole,
So its by faith they plead, for they know not sure,
But their clients were ground through the mill before,
And of course this time when their suit is ground,
Not a ragged fee in their coffer's found.
   When the physician leaves his home so warm,
All capped and mailed in fur against the storm,
Does he know indeed that his money's sure?
Or the guerdon he books time will secure?
Does he know the nostrums he will prescribe—
On which his patients so blindly confide—
Of cob web, rag-weed, or chamomile,
Will heal up their maladies sound and well?
Knows he—if death don't keep pace with his speed—
That the monster will not outstrip his steed?
Nay, he's no preknowledge of all these things,
Though of his ambition they're all the springs.
So the doctor drives his profession by faith,

Eclectic, Homeopathic, or Allopath.
As he goes out healing how can he tell
But that his profession's enormous bill
Has picked the poor patient's very last dime,
Or helped him out of the troubles of time ?
That the doctor's pale horse had pawed and neighed
So oft by the gate where the sick man staid,
That, coming today he'll not be at home.
Yet onward he rides, and by faith alone.
So the preacher goes forth by faith in God,
To publish the grace of His living Word.
The teacher, statesman and politician,
All chase their phantom on faith's condition.
Not a merchant knows when investing means,
Whether fortune 1 ink, or exceed his dreams.
So he buys by faith on a truth supposed,
Only known a truth when the stock is closed.
In all the surging sea of human life,
In all the drive and rush of business strife,
From the great "Wall Street," to the suburb shop,
All the markets piled with the round earth's crop.
Every mart of trade, every business line,
All that's grown or made on the shores of time,
Is raised, made, shipped, bought, sold and consumed by
And unmoved by faith all would starve to death. [faith.
Not a living man would rise from his seat,

Not another step ever take his feet,
Did he not have faith that his body is blest
With might to respond to his mind's behest.
As the Lord by faith framed the world withal,
So by faith all live on this mundane ball.

# THE GROUND OF FAITH.

THE evidences that array themselves in support of any proposition are the ground or basis of faith in that proposition. Where a sufficient amount of evidence to sustain a proposition is lacking, the mind cannot give assent to it, nor the will act upon it with assurance. But when the evidences are strong and conclusive, the mind must give assent, and yet the will, through counter attractions and disinclinations, may even then withhold action. So we have placed evidence as the ground of faith, but motive the cause of its action. As a person cannot walk without a basis to walk on, but may, or may not, as he shall elect, with a basis; so without evidence faith cannot proceed, but with it, can, if the person choose, or remain inactive if he so determine.

Under this head we will confine ourself to the faith of the Gospel, and can only take time to call attention to a few facts, of all the multitude of evidences of the Divine Revelation.

The interposition of a supernatural fire, which drove the Emperor Julian's workmen from the site of the temple, we refer to in this connection, is a fact clearly recorded in history. Ambrose, Chrysostom, and other Christian writers of that age, and Marcellinus a Pagan writer, recorded the fact, and Gibbon the noted infidel historian, who never misses an opportunity to obscure the sacred truth, refers to the instance in his history of Rome, and does not call it in question.

# THE GROUND OF FAITH.

WE stand all amazed mid the lights that shine
Within and without of the Book Divine,
And ten thousand objects that round us crowd,
All speaking in harmony clear and loud,
The Bible! dear Bible! the Book of love!
Is no earthly production; but Heaven above
Hath kindled its fire and lit up its page
With hope for the lost, both simple and sage.
   To a creature with eyes, this world is bright
With the rays of the sun from morn 'till night,
Him no arguments need to be given,
To prove the genial beams of heaven.
But to one born blind, what a task it were
For the wisdom of a philosopher.
To convey one proof of the fact of light,
Without the power to furnish him sight.
All the rapturous scenes in the earth or sky,
Or the living canvas of a Monkacsy,
Cannot pierce his veil with the faintest gleam,
Or awake in his mind a single dream.

So it comes to us as a thankless thing
That some proofs of the Bible we should sing,
For the saint who lives in the  perfect light,
And the sinner too, with a vision slight, ,
Need not our taper to behold the sun.
While light for self blinded, alas! there's none.
It seems detraction from the truth of Heaven,
That evidence yet must needs be given,
To prove this Book is the voice of the Blest,
Fact clearly evinced as that we exist.
But critics and fools in their folly stark,
Because their hearts and their deeds were evil and
Have scanned this footstool of God all around, [dark
And excavated the depth of the ground.
To find in its dark deep chambers a clue
To its origin, and perchance o'erthrow
The record Creative Wisdom's given,
In the ancient Book of the God of Heaven.
Some hidden tally in this rock-ribbed clod,
That disagrees with the Bible of God.
So these "free thinkers"—free to thoughts of evil—
Might set up a claim, as did the devil,
The world's their own, and they made it withal,
Or at least discovered t'was'nt made at all.
So all right and title of God o'er thrown,
They swear by high Heaven this world's their own.

But what have the restless scientists found,
And agreed upon as the facts profound?
Both devout and infidel all set forth
Five gen'ral stratas comprising the earth;
Each thought to denote a cycle of years,
In the earth's formation, e'er man appears.
But who is able to arise and say
God could not have formed it all in a day,
Or in the six days of the true Genesis?
Could He not have fashioned it just as't is,
All stratumed through, and in fossel disguised,
To bring to naught the wisdom of the wise?
But should the past ages have 'lapsed indeed,
On which the scientists are much agreed,   ·
"The BEGINNING," that breaks the silence first,
And spans the unlimited cycles past,
Has ample room for the ages unknown,
Through which it is claimed our planet has grown·
From silent chaos to an Eden land.
Whether ages long had a moulding hand
On the substance of this terrestrial clod,
Ere the six days work of Almighty God;
Or whether those days themselves were cycles vast
Or were solar days, what's the odds at last?
In  these leading facts however accord
Both youthful science and the Old Record.

First, the creative work in Genesis,
Was extended, not simultaneous.
Geology, having explored the earth,
Comes up from the depths and, behold! sets forth
The fact likewise of the time's extension
In the rocky annals of creation.
  And a second point in the Book of Truth,
Is, the world came not by a gradual growth;
But by the fiat of Eternal Mind,
It was formed in epochs, each well defined
As a day with a silent night between.
And so to the stratas that intervene
Betwixt the successive epochal rounds,
Geology points, as sufficient grounds
To confirm the Book of Eternal worth.
Again, in the origin of this earth,
The leaves of nature with the Book agree,
That just five stages fill its history.
And in their order, and the nature of each,
Neither doth the other a word impeach.
The earth was at first "without form and void;"
'Tis said in the ancient inspired Word.
We open the volumes of science and, lo!
The original earth was chaos too.
Both pictures do perfectly coincide,
The "*Azoic age*," and "the earth yet void."

Next, in the record that God has given,
The land and the sea : part were driven,
And the earth yielded grass, herb, seed and tree.
With this again all science will agree.
Chaos first, and next vegetation,
Ascends the scale of true Revelation.
Then waters brought forth fish, and did appear
Reptiles, "moving creatures," "fowls of the air."
Now turning to the charts of geology,
We see how they're forced into harmony
With the grand old Book of the Christian's trust.
How the learned have seen in the very dust,
And throughout the frame of this globe they find,
The finger marks of the very same Mind
That moved the writings of sacred annals.
'Twixt vegetation, and age of mammals,
The "*Mezoic and Paleozoic*" stands,
Marked by the reptile life, and tribe of fins.
So Heaven above has chronicaled true,
And so read the stratas of earth below.
Next we ascend to the animal plain;
Where the cattle and beasts of the earth did reign.
These all came forth in the Bible story,
Between the fish and the crowning glory,
Of the workmanship of the Great I AM.
Just where they're placed in the scientist's plan;

The "*Cenozoic*" mammals of all kind,
Just before we come to the age of mind.
    And the last of all, in the Christian's creed,
And in the science of the earth we tread,
Lo! man was formed and made a living soul.
Mighty lord of earth, from pole to pole.
So, on the drip-stone of each succeeding stage,
God has carved a proof of the sacred page.
Wonderful! wonderful!! coincidence,
In the voice of nature and that of grace!
Ah! 'Tis the same voice that speaks with compassion
In the pure Volume of Inspiration.
And thunders aloud in the riven clouds,
Or sings soft vespers when the evening shrouds
The closing day in holy curtains round,
And breathes a solemn awe, as hushed each sound
Of busy toil-   The voice of Majesty,
That roars anon upon the billowed sea.
The music universal nature rings
Is the sweet anthem that the Bible sings.
And the God of nature—let wisdom trace—
Is the God of the Bible, God of grace.


    A thousand facts foretold on the pages
Of this Great Book, in the lapse of ages
Have ceased to speak as slighted prophecy,

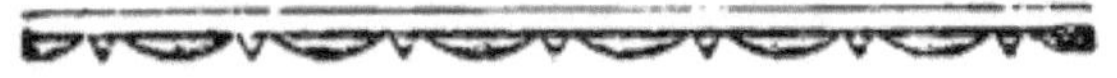

And have entered the annals of history.
In all these predictions Truth put forth
A challenge before the monarch's of earth,
And the forces of hell and sin combined,
To overthrow what the prophets divined.
Tho' the kingdoms arose and skeptics railed,
Not a jot or title has ever failed.
What the Wonderful Volume pre-declares
Of cities and nations, all hist'ry bears
Its faithful record, that, so far as due,
All has come to pass most strikingly true.
One beautiful instance we sing alone
Should cast every skeptic in silence down,
With his mouth in the dust, a penitent,
His vulgar speeches and deeds to repent.
  In the Gospel of Christ, the true God-man,
On the holy City Jerusalem,
Predicted that she in ages to come,
Should furnish no Jew a sheltering home.
"Till the times of the Gentiles be complete,
'She must be trodden 'neath the Gentile's feet.
A judgment no human sagacity
Would ever have ventured to prophesy.
But the mouth of the Lord hath spoken it,
And who shall be able to interdict.
What! this indefeasible race denied

Access to the place of their sacred pride?
Behold the King of Kings and Lord of Lords
Inclines the powers that be to fill His words.
So the Romans came as a storm of woe
And leveled the city in ruins low.
Eleven hundred thousand Hebrews met
Death in the valley of Jehoshaphat.
And every Jew that survived on earth
Was hence prohibited on pain of death
To enter, or even to look upon
Their down-trodden City Jerusalem.
A "hissing," and "proverb," in slavery sold,
They filled up the measure that seers foretold.
After fifty years under Egypt's yoke
The Emp'ror Adrain, their souls to provoke,
Rebuilded the city in Roman style
All its sacred places did much defile.
He profaned the temple's most awful mound
By erecting upon its sacred ground,
And from its honored stones, a theatre
With a heathen temple to Jupiter.
And to show the poor Jews the nation's hate,
Carved a marble swine just o'er each gate,
In the wall of the city round about.
This inflamed the blood of the Jews devout.
And through Barchobebas, a false Messiah.

To retake the City they did conspire.
A mighty army, in desperate wrath,
Resolved on the City, or suffer death.
But the words of Jesus against them stood,
And in vain they battled and shed their blood.
Five hundred and eighty thousand, with great
Barchobebas their leader, met their fate.
And the Roman guards for centuries round
Shut out every Jew from the sacred ground.
Nor dared he yet creep o'er the rubbish there,
To see and bewail his Zion so dear.

   But should the flaming sword of earthly law
From the gates of that City once withdraw,
Would not that people in eagerness come
From every nation to their ancient home?
Yea, and dig from the earth each temple-stone,
If favored indeed by some mighty Throne.
And so they were.   A monarch's mighty mace
Assayed to restore to the Jews their place.
A nephew of the Christian Constantine,
Was Julian, and he himself had been
A nominal Christian in early youth,
But, apostatizing, he held the truth
In wicked abhorrence, and in his hate
Resolved to utterly annihilate,
And root out of the earth the Christian name.

So through his empire he published a ban
That all the stupid Pagan deities,
Where the gods of his kingdom, and to these
Were temples reared up, while the Christian  cause
Was hindered by subtile proscriptive laws.
He, by his observation and research,
Having learned, a fruitful seed of the Church,
Is the blood and ashes of martyred saints,
Held his pent rancor under wise restraints.
If 'gainst the Christian structure he'd prevail,
Its very foundation he must assail.
He found no flaw in the ethics of love
That our Savior taught; nor could he disprove
That the body of ancient prophecy,
All had centered in Him so perfectly.
The prophetic picture that Jesus drew,
Over three hundred years had sealed it true.
And Julian knew that the Lord had said,
The feet of the Gentiles alone should tread
The streets of the City where God had dwelt,
'Till the time of the Gentiles be fulfilled.
"Not so," said the sagacious Emperor,
"This Galileean's word shall stand no more.
"By the might of my gods, and kingdom great,
"By my army of Pagans, filled with hate,
"And by the pent up zeal of every Jew,

"I swear this prediction shall prove untrue.
"I know how the Israelite bosom's burn
"With love for their City, and would return,
"And dig from the dust all her sacred stones,
"And rebuild the place of their ancient homes.
"I'll remove the bars that have shut them out,
"And open the way for the Jews, devout.
"And welcome them back from the nations round,
"To build their temple on its ancient ground.
"So Jerusalem, all the world shall see,
"The home of that nation henceforth shall be."
Forth went the tidings in the Monarch's name
So the Jews arose, and in ardor came,
And entered with awe on the sacred spot,
Their gold and silver in abundance brought,
And in the wildest enthusiasm,
Began to search for the old foundation,
Of the holy palace, in ruin laid.
The wealthy brought silver pick and spade,
And so devoted were Jewish females,
That they bore off rubbish in silken veils.
What sanguine raptures inspired all the throng,
As they cleared the debris with shout and song.
Great Jewish zeal, with the iron empire,
And all heathen gods, and devils conspire,
With millions of gold to second their plan,

Must surely succeed at Jerusalem;
And so destroy the only foundation
Of hope for a world in sin's perdition.
Must prove a default in the Book of love,
And reduce our Lord to a level with Jove.
What a crisis this for the world has been!
What a vantage ground for the skeptic's pen!
There was no earthly power as hitherto,
To guard that site against the zealous Jew.
A throne Universal is on their side,
The provincial governor, strong beside.
So the Bible must fail if it's a farce,
Having no other arm but its own Source
To maintain its honor in this great test,
Unshaken and worthy the Christian's trust.
If God be God, He must now interpose
Or suffer His truth o'erthrown by His foes.
But look! look!! the workers all flee amazed.
Lo! o'er their heads a fiery tempest blazed.
An earthquake shakes the ground beneath their feet,
And dreadful balls of fire upward leap
From beneath the walls, scorching unto death
Some that wrought: others fled the angry breath.
When the elements hushed their dreadful blast
The zealots resumed their defiant task.
But were again and again compelled to run

From the fiery breath of the Holy One.
Repulsed and alarmed by Jehovah's ire,
They fled from the place of ominous fire.
And abandoned the hope of proving vain
The words that were spoken in Heaven's name.
  Then to Persia the apostate pressed on
In hope of conquest for his pagan crown.
But fell in battle by a Persian lance,
And conscious that fate had taken his chance,
A palm of his blood in the air he cast,
While conscience smit, his dying lips confessed,
"O *Galilean!* thou hast conquered!"
'Twas a name of reproach he had conferred
On all who in the Christian faith then lived.
So he died, but the Christian cause survived;
And yet survives;  her mighty truth yet saves,
While her foes have gone to dishonored graves.
  Soon came the Turks and took the holy land,
And held it 'neath Mahometan command,
Down through the centuries until this day.
Save the ninety years, when crusaders sway—
More cruel even than the Caliph's rule—
Assayed to wipe the Jews from God's footstool.
So then the bold words of the prophet Christ,
For eighteen hundred years have stood the test.
And now, while the Gentile sects are falling

Into darkness, and the angels calling,
All the living forth from her corruption,
And from her awful decreed consumption,
When, in fact, the gentile's day is waning,
And the time is due for the Jew's returning,
Behold! a wealthy man* of providence,
Secures abundant opening through the fence
Of Islam's government, and, lo! they come!
Jews come, and make Jerusalem their home.

Was this all an accident?   Who believes
That chance has filled up eighteen centuries
Of prophecy, the most improbable,
Believes a lie however palpable,
Because for truth he has no relish,
All his bent and habitudes so dev'lish.

Not only prophecies all harmonize
With historic facts, but they synchronize
With each other in beautiful accord.
One point we cite.   The words of Christ the Lord †
Place the point of the Gentile's closing time
At the Jews returning home to Palestine.
And His Apostle‡ makes their fullness end
When the Jews shall cease to grope, lost and blind.
Then these two signals of the same event,
Must with each other be coincident.

*Rothschild.       †Luke 21: 24.      ‡Rom. 11: 25.

And, lo! their co-occurrence in these years
A striking truth this generation bears.
While many thousand Jews regain a blest
Home in Palestine, thousands also rest
Their hopes on Him their fathers crucified.
A proof that time is in its even-tide.
A solemn warning to the Gentile world
That grace and love, long trodden down and foiled,
Now concentrate in the Church their glowing,
And, insulted, withdraw their gentle wooing
And leave the nations in delusive coil.
To sin and hell an everlasting spoil.
   Not only can we trace upon the leaves
Of nature, and historical archives,
Many thousand lines of truth, harmonic,
That rebuke the madness of the skeptic,
And set their seal and evidence, sublime,
Confirming inspiration's Book Divine;
But, turning to the inner soul and mind,
What, in all the realm of thought do we find,
Or where, in our spirit's wonderful throne,
Is there one principle that does not own,
And feel the need of a revelation
From God, the Author of all creation?
And every truth in the Bible's plan
A counterpart finds in the soul of man.

One element deep in the human breast
Is hope, which anchors in a future, blest.
It many objects here on earth desrcies,
But sees beyond this world its crowning prize.
As a faculty of immortal soul,
Immortality is its final goal.
Would the Maker of all in man create
Appetence for a bright and future state,
And make for that want no sure provision?
Or if provide. withhold the condition
Of gaining the home of hope's fruition?
Thus mocking the wants of His own creation.
And such were the case if no guide were given
To light up indwelling hopes of Heaven.
  Again, we do most assuredly draw
That man was fashioned a subject of law.
For, lo! it is written deep in his soul,
The will of his Maker should all control.
And his actions, he feels and knows within
Are pleasing to God, or presumptuous sin.
The principle of right and wrong reveals
Itself within our soul, but yet it feels
Dependent on its Author for the light,
To discriminate 'twixt wrong and right.
Would God implant responsibility.
And leave man grope in dread uncertainty,

Perplexed through life with gloomy fears that he
With Heaven's will were out of harmony,
And yet confer on him no standard by
Which obedience could his conscience satisfy?
Nay, the clear sense of moral quality,
And the universal fear of penalty,
Incorporated in the human mind,
With many thousand other facts combined,
Prove man was made for revelation's beam,
And that this sacred Book's inspired for him.
In the ambient skies, earth, and awful main,
Where e'er we cast an eye with honest aim,
And unperverted reason, lo! appear
Endorsements of the Book good men revere.
Truly "the Heavens declare thy Glory,"
And all earth bespeaks Redemption's story.
Yea on the tablets of our inner being
Are written lines with this volume agreeing.
  And now the God of inspiration stands,
And points throughout the earth to Bible lands,
And, though His truth has been by creeds obscured,
And from the factious sects hath more endured
Than from the heathen's rage and skeptic's sneer,
Yet no unbibled lands with them compare.
  Ah! the Truth is yet by miracles confirmed,
What mighty works of grace stout hearts have turned

And wills, like iron shafts inflexible
Before the powers of earth, yet meekly fall
At the feet of Christ, neath His Gospel's sway,
When published through some pure, but feeble clay.
What hand but the Almighty could transmute
Soul, mind and body, sunk beneath the brute,
Profane, and debauched, a demonized dread,
To a loving saint, washed, and raised from the dead?
Yea! who else but the Infinite Author
Of man's prime holiness, is greater
Than its despoiler, and doth raise again
His soul to its pure primeval plain?
We need not speak of the healing power,
That rescues the body in sickness' hour.
That raises the sick from the bed of pain,
Gives sight to the blind, and strength to the lame.
These kind touches of love we see,
So common in evening's effulgency.
While stamping truth on the living story,
They're trivial beside the grace and glory,
That quicken the soul and the life of men,
From the shades of hell, to a heaven begun.
And such are the fruits of an honest trust
In the Book beloved by the pure and just.
Ah! let reason, sense and candor reply,
Do such result from believing a lie?

Are fruits so gentle, so lovely and good
Plucked from a tree that is only a fraud?
All they that do rashly this Volume assail,
And call it a false and fabulous tale,
Have stultified reason and good sense too,
Made falsehood the mother of all virtue,
And an impostor, they are forced to confess
Only can save us, can comfort and bless.
O skeptic! thy witcheries dark as the night,
Spring from an instilled hatred of the light.
And all your strained arguments and research
To dispose of God, His Bible and Church
But prove that God is ; for if otherwise
Naught would exist to chafe your energies
Into such restless effort to disprove
His being, and undermined His Book of love.
So that which you labor to overthrow,
You, in mental science, prove to be true.
Poor slaves ! driven by doubts and fears
Through barren wastes of uncertainties !
Slaves to an empty creed you wish were true,
But would give all the world if you but knew.
But the Christian knows whom he hath believed,
And the conscious knowledge of truth received.
   "He is the freeman whom the truth makes free,
And all are slaves beside.  There's not a chain

That hellish foes confederate for his harm
Can wind around him, but he casts it off
With as much ease as Samson his green withes.
He looks abroad into the varied field
Of nature, and though poor perhaps, compared
With those whose mansions glitter in his sight,
Calls the delightful scenery all his own.
His are the mountains, and the valleys his,
And the resplendent rivers.   His to enjoy
With a propriety that none can feel,
But who, with filial confidence inspired,
Can lift to heaven an unpresumptuous eye,
And smiling say—" My Father made them all!"
Are they not his by a peculiar right,
And by an emphasis of interest his,
Whose eye they fill with tears of holy joy,
Whose heart with praise, and whose exalted mind
With worthy thoughts of that unwearied love
That plann'd, and built, and still upholds a world
So clothed with beauty, for rebellious man?
Yes—ye may fill your garners, ye that reap
The loaded soil, and ye may waste much good
In senseless riot ; but ye will not find,
In feast or in the chase, in song or dance,
A liberty like his, who unimpeach'd
Of usurpation, and to no man's wrong,

Appropriates nature as his Father's work,
And has a richer use of yours, than you.
He is indeed a freeman; free by birth
Of no mean city, plann'd or e'er the hills
Were built, the fountains open'd, or the sea
With all its roaring multitude of waves.
His freedom is the same in every state;
And no condition of this changeful life,
So manifold in cares, whose every day
Brings its own evil with it, makes it less:
For he has wings that neither sickness, pain,
Nor penury can cripple or confine.
No nook so narrow but he spreads them there
With ease, and is at large.   The oppressor holds
His body bound, but knows not what a range
His spirit takes, unconscious of a chain,
And that to bind him is a vain attempt
Whom God delights in, and in whom He dwells.
   "Acquaint thyself with God, if thou wouldst taste
His works.   Admitted once to His embrace,
Thou shalt perceive that thou wast blind before;
Thine eye shall be instructed, and thine heart,
Made pure, shall relish with divine delight
Till then unfelt, what hands divine have wrought.
Brutes graze the mountain-top with faces prone
And eyes intent upon the scanty herb

It yields them; or, recumbent on its brow,
Ruminate heedless of the scene outspread
Beneath, beyond, and stretching far away
From inland regions to the distant main.
Man views it and admires, but rests content
With what he views. The landscape has his praise,
But not its Author. Unconcern'd who form'd
The paradise he sees, he finds it such,
And such well-pleas'd to find it, asks no more.
Not so the mind that has been touch'd from Heaven,
And in the school of sacred wisdom taught
To read His wonders, in whose thought the world,
Fair as it is, existed ere it was.
Not for its own sake merely, but for His
Much more who fashion'd it, he gives it praise;
Praise that from earth resulting as it ought
To earth's acknowledged Sovereign, finds at once
Its only just proprietor in Him.

     "Tell me, ye shining hosts
That navigate a sea that knows no storms,
Beneath a vault unsullied with a cloud,
If from your elevation, whence ye view
Distinctly scenes invisible to man.
And systems of whose birth no tidings yet
Have reach'd this nether world, ye spy a race

Favor'd as ours, transgressors from the womb,
And hasting to a grave, yet doom'd to rise,
And to possess a brighter heaven than yours?
As one who long detained on foreign shores
Pants to return, and when he sees afar
His country's weather-bleach'd and batter'd rocks,
From the green wave emerging, darts an eye
Radiant with joy towards the happy land;
So I  With animated hopes behold,
And many an aching wish, your beamy fires,
That show like beacons in the blue abyss,
Ordained to guide the embodied spirit home,
From toilsome life to never-ending rest.
Love kindles as I gaze.  I feel desires
That give assurance of their own success,
And that infused from Heaven must thither tend."
  "So reads he nature whom the lamp of truth
Illuminates.  Thy lamp, mysterious Word!
Which whoso sees no longer wanders lost
With intellects bemazed in endless doubt,
But runs the road of wisdom.  Thou hast built,
With means that were not till by Thee employ'd,
Worlds that had never been hadst Thou in strength
been less, or less benevolent than strong.
They are Thy witnesses, who speak Thy power
And goodness infinite, but speak in ears

That hear not, or receive not their report.
In vain Thy creatures testify of Thee
Till Thou proclaim Thyself.   Theirs is indeed
A teaching voice; but 'tis the praise of Thine
That whom it teaches it makes prompt to learn,
And with the boon gives talents for its use.
Till Thou art heard, imaginations vain
Possess the heart, and fables false as hell,
Yet deem'd oracular, lure down to death
The uninform'd and heedless souls of men.
We give to Chance, blind Chance, ourselves as blind,
The glory of Thy work, which yet appears
Perfect and unimpeachable of blame,
Challenging human scrutiny, and proved
Then skilful most when most severely judged.
But Chance is not; or is not where thou reign'st:
Thy providence forbids that fickle power
(If power she be that works but to confound)
To mix her wild vagaries with Thy laws.
Yet thus we dote, refusing while we can
Instruction, and inventing to ourselves
Gods such as guilt makes welcome; gods that sleep,
Or disregard our follies, or that sit
Amused spectators of this bustling stage.
Thee we reject, unable to abide
Thy purity, till pure as Thou art pure,,

Made such by Thee, we love Thee for that cause
For which we shun   and hated Thee before.
Then we are free: then liberty like day,
Breaks on the soul, and by a flash from Heaven
Fires all the faculties with glorious joy.
A voice is heard that mortal ears hear not
Till Thou hast touched them; 'tis the voice of song,
A loud Hosanna sent from all Thy works,
Which he that hears it with a shout repeats,
And adds his rapture to the general praise.
In that blest moment, Nature, throwing wide
Her veil opaque, discloses with a smile
The Author of her beauties, who, retired
Behind His own creation, works unseen
By the impure, and hears His power denied.
Thou art the source and centre of all minds,
Their only point of rest, eternal Word!
From Thee departing, they are lost and rove
At random, without honor, hope, or peace.
From Thee is all that soothes the life of man,
His high endeavor, and his glad success,
His strength to suffer, and his will to serve.
But oh, Thou bounteous Giver of all good,
Thou art of all Thy gifts Thyself the crown!
Give what Thou canst, without Thee we are poor;
And with Thee rich, take what thou wilt away."*

*Cowper.

# FAITH WORKS BY LOVE.

## *It is a voluntary action incited by motives.*

And is therefore moral'y right or wrong, according to whether the act springs from a good or bad motive

Two prominent elements of faith we wish to bring out in this section; namely, that faith is a voluntary act of the will, and that moral quality is attached to the act of faith.

"Faith works by love," only acts when the motives and affections incline the action. The motives for or against an action, are perfectly distinct from the evidences for or against it. It is also a fact that persons act on a proposition, with but little evidence in its favor, and a strong preponderance of evidence against it, when the action is in the direction of their ruling desires. Also they refuse to believe when there is an overwhelming degree of evidence; because they do not love the proposition. If the heart and mind are wicked and selfish, they will believe a lie and act accordingly, carefully shunning the evidences that expose the lie. At the same time they will disbelieve the truth that stands opposite to the cherished lie though they must labor to keep their eyes closed to the abundant evidences that prove it truth. Or in scripture language, "they will not come to the light because they love darkness," and "because their deeds are evil." So the beliefs in which a man lives in this world, chiefly depend upon the state of his heart.

It is a morally good act to believe and act upon that which is a blessing to ourselves and our fellows. It is a wicked faith that springs from the promptings of sin and selfishness. And since the religion of Christ is so manifestly the source of all true happiness, nothing but wickedness of heart could lead men to disbelieve it. Therefore he that believeth not shall be damned.

# FAITH WORKS BY LOVE.

A TRUTH may gain assent against the will,
But if the mind is all rebellious still,
From that no act of faith will yet proceed,
Until the heart embrace that truth indeed.
Though light may force conviction on the mind,
That is not faith; but when the heart's inclined
By an honest purpose to relinquish
All its idols for the truth to purchase,
The will and intellect in candor weigh
The evidences that in force array
Themselves upon the side of truth, and so
Acquaints himself with facts that hitherto
He cared not, or even willed not to see,
Now, loving truth, acts on it willingly.
This is faith; an act of free volition,
If on Christ, resulting in salvation.
He chose to scan the facts that underlay
Supposed truth, willed to do it honestly,
And when the mind was forced to give assent,
The will's prerogative was to consent,

Or still refuse to act upon the right,
Which, loving darkness rather than the light,
He'd have done in spite of all conviction.
Some much cherished lie, controling action.
And when the mind perceives clear evidence
Of truth, but acts not on the premises;
Because he chooses not to love the same,
Confused and guilty, he begins to feign
Excuses for not acting in the right,
Yea! wishes that the facts were out of sight,
Invites the devil in to help him doubt,
Until the light of truth is all shut out.
The sin-beclouded mind, and no surprise,
He's given up to credit satan's lies:
And "having pleasure in unrighteousness,"
Falls in a maze of scoffing wickedness.

So, in all the compass of its actions,
If in earth or Heaven's propositions,
Believing truth, or acting on a lie,
Faith acts from choice and not compulsory.
But when it springs from evidences clear,
And is inspired by motives good and pure,
'Tis easy, graceful as the water's flow,
Approved within, and blest with reason's glow.
Not so the faith that's refuged in a lie;
All its supports are seen by evil eye.

Its prompting motive som ungodly lust,
'Tis a forced, restless, and distorted trust.
"Faith works by love."   Like the mighty leaven,
Is powerless until some heat is given.
Though in the meal, it is yet motionless
Until some genial warmth to action bless.
So God hath planted in each human soul,
Elements of faith that would make him whole,
Were they not held in paralyzed suspense,
By love of sin and vile concupiscence.
But which, as soon as love of truth obtains
Candid place within the heart and brains,
Will warm that germ of life to work in him
A mighty transformation from all sin.
Faith works *on truth*, but only works *by love*.
Inspired by love great mountains it can move.
Yea, all things are possible, in God's name,
To him whose faith is fired by Heaven's flame.
The latent faith of sinners cannot flow;
Because unthawed by love of truth: and so
That faith distorted to believe a lie,
Can have no place where now the "evil eye"
Is gone, and where no love at all remains
For any gilded falsehood hell ordains.
So faith will follow where affections lead,
Whether love of truth, or a sensual greed.

Awaits the moving of our inward bent,
And works according to the hearts consent.
Works by love, be it love of God or sin;
Works out in life whatever dwells within.
No marvel then "the fool hath said in heart—
And greater fools their shocking thoughts impart
There is no God."   No god but self they trust;
Because they love no god but selfish lust.
"No God!" Since faith can only work by love,
It cannot move toward the throne above,
While all the mind is filled with base desire
The heart with hellish lust is set on fire.

Because affection's throne is in the heart,
Mere intellectual faith can't life impart.
Since Faith can only work by love indeed,
Its work must from the seat of love proceed.
So if the gift of God men would receive,
They must repent, and with the heart believe.
Here rise the only mountains that obtrude
Between the sinner and his faith in God.
These mountains, which his love for sin create
Will quickly vanish when he turns to hate
The sin and selfishness that kill his soul,
And gives the love of truth his heart's control.
So will all sinners find in Judgment's day
They loved a lie, and turned from truth away.

Sowed to lust and sin by free volition,
And must reap their own in dark perdition.
While the redeemed, though conscious of the fact
Their faith in God was all a free will act,
In all justice, cannot to that ascribe
Any merit, but to the Crucified
Give all glory, who died and shed His blood
To open mercy's passage back to God.
No praise to him who takes a gracious boon,
All praise to Him who bought it in the tomb.

# WHAT DOES FAITH WORK?

HERE all the infinite range of faith's triumphs and achievements lays open before us. Every noble and heroic deed on the pages of sacred and profane history offers itself as an answer to the question. But as time hastens us to a close, we can only let a few points respond.

# WHAT DOES FAITH WORK?

Before the glorious Sun and Moon were formed,
Or a single star immensity adorned,
God, "who inhabiteth eternity,"
In love and wisdom chose that there should be
Material worlds throughout His boundless space,
That He might bless creation with His grace.
And, conscious of His own Omnipotence,
Believed Himself in power to call them hence.
To speak into being shining orbs so fair,
Make substances from naught that did appear.
He spake.   And "through His faith the worlds were
      framed.'
Their glorious song the power of faith proclaimed.
And yet they seem in harmony to swell
This song, "All things by faith are possible."
By faith God spake, and light from darkness shone
So in the soul, where sinful night hath thrown
The dismal shades of hell, and black despair,
Salvation, grasped by faith, shines sweetly there.
Yea! shines a crystal morn, a peaceful dawn,
A day of bliss whose Sun shall ne'er go down.

Faith works knowledge, unbars the iron doors,
That hold in sacred trust her golden stores.
When erst our eye the teacher's pointer met
On the first letter of the Alphabet,
In gentle loving tone we heard him say
Its name, and we by faith responded, "A."
Then one by one, pronouncing as he did,
Until the Alphabet throughout was said.
And repeating daily, 'till all were learned,
We, by faith, this first stock of knowledge earned.
But an urchin deeply dipped in skeptic dye,
Would doubtless face the teacher and deny.
Would not receive from any one that knew,
Until within himself he'd found it true.
So skeptic logic would dispense with schools,
And leave the world inhabited by fools.
But nay, a child is not of sense so void,
As not to judge the man that is employed
To teach is taught, and will not him misguide:
So does implicitly in him confide.
Accepts each lesson on the teacher's trust,
And turns to knowledge what was faith at first.
As he ascends upon the steps of lore,
Each lesson learned by faith adds to his store,
Of knowledge, which is capital increased,
Enabling faith more largely to invest.

As we by faith our wisdom's fund acquire, '
So knowledge doth in turn our faith inspire.
And from these facts we draw an evidence
That unbelief proceeds from ignorance:
While ignorance holds sway through unbelief.
These keep each, and possessor dumb and deaf.
For he that believeth nothing 'till he knows,
Knows nothing, and his stupid eyes shall close
On life in desolation's emptiness.
Yet one exception we would here confess.
He may have picked up, on the shores of time,
A few trifling shells, and indeed a fine
Pearl or two, by sheer accident.
But all thus gathered were incompetent
To avert a gen'ral desolation
Of the stagnant world in every nation.
Faith works by love, and knowledge is its hire.
'Twas faith that did that sailors heart inspire
With persevering plea from throne to throne,
For aid to navigate the seas unknown.
Hung seven years upon the court of Spain.
Bluffed in Portugal, England' France, his plan
Still burned with unmitigated ferver,
Till his suit obtained the Spanish favor.
He launched by faith, undaunted by the sneers
Of all the world.  Endured by faith the fears,

The threats, and murmurs of his fellows,
Seeing land by faith, beyond the billows.
And faith held on until it turned to sight,
Brought the knowledge of a new world to light.
    'Twas faith sent Franklin's kite the clouds amid
To bottle secrets that before were hid :
She caught the swift lightnings that rend the skies,
And brought knowledge for man to utilize.
Faith launched the mighty steam-boat on the main,
Put wings of lightning on the flying train.
Yea, all the triumphs of inventive skill,
Were wrought by faith, through muscle, mind and
And, like the rolling billows of the deep,     [will.
Have laid new pearls of knowledge at our feet.
But the faith that worketh information,
Must put forth upon a proposition
That is true ; or else no acquisition
Of wealth or wisdom can award its action.
Had God ne'er made this western Continent,
A faith that searched would unrequited went.
So the Atheist believes there is no God.
Believes, but lives through life beneath the fog
Of painful haunting dark uncertainty ;
Yet blind ; because believing in a lie.
The infidel, through worldly lust and pride,
Believes the Bible is a spurious guide.

But his faith ne'er works a demonstration,
'Till his eyes are opened in perdition.
So trusting lies dispels no ignorance,
But leaves the soul drift on in inference.
True there will yet be a demonstration
Of skeptic's faith, but information
Derived will come too late to profit by,
Save judgment's cure of infidelity.

A contrite soul knows not what God will do,
But, promised pardon, he believes it true.
He bows, repents, prays, in his heart believes,
And, lo! that instant pardoning grace receives.
He but grasped a truthful proposition,
And *faith* wrought "*the knowledge of salvation!*"
Ere long he feels a hunger yet within,
And conscious evil bents inflict a sting.
He hears the testimony of the pure,
And hungers for the fulness more and more.
"Be ye holy," perfect as your Father,"
These, and many scriptures blend together,
In sweet provisions for that perfect love
His soul intensely thirsts and waits to prove.
He believes, dies to sin, and pays the price,
And Heaven seals the perfect sacrifice.
Seals it with the Spirit's testimony,
Crying, "Holy!" "Holy!!" Soul and body.

Here faith again is turned to glorious sight;
An inward knowledge that the soul is white.
In every fiber speaks the voice of God,
All "Holy!" "Holy!!" through the precious blood.
No more he hopes, believes, the promise true;
But knows and feels it burning through and through.
So faith brings knowledge in the things Divine
As clear, yea, more sure, than in things of time.
Need there be an unbelieving sinner,
With a book of thirty thousand ever
Open promises, for any one to test?
Let some great Genius claim that he were blest
With over thirty thousand recipes,
That cover all our deep necessities.
Healing for the sick, and sight for the blind;
Hearing for the deaf, comfort to the mind.
A balm to heal the wounded soul from sin.
Extract from guilt and death their bitter sting.
Give strength to the weak, rest from every care,
And joy to the heart long chained in despair.
A remedy sure for each mortal woe,
For passions infernal that rage and glow.
Give blessings just suited to every need,
On conditions all easy and just indeed.
Why should a mortal then suffer in pain,
And leave untested such wonderful claim?

If the gracious announcements should be so,
'Twere your int'rest to test and prove them true.
Or if a fraud, why not test it and know,
Its falsehood by trial would readily show.
    And, lo! such a Benefactor has come!
An angel of mercy from Heaven's throne,
With healing in His wings to earth descends,
And, Behold! in our midst He meekly stands,
Crying, "Come unto me; sad hearts I will gladden.
"Come all ye weary and heavy laden.
"Come, ye shall find rest for your troubled soul,
"Your griefs I'll carry, broken hearts make whole.
"And the foes of thy soul I will destroy,
"Give beauty for ashes; the oil of Joy
"For thy mourning, and the garment of praise;
"And great peace shall attend thy pilgrim days.
"Yea more than thine eye of fancy can see,
"If thou wilt believe and come unto me,
"Without money or price, I will do for thee.
"More?  Yea, exceedingly abundantly."
Thus the thirty one thousand promises
Of His Heavenly Book do advertise.
Why in perplexity linger to know
If these gracious tidings be true or no?
See, every promise doth open a door
Thee to enter and for thyself explore.

His honor is staked upon every word.
On each promise must stand or fall the Lord.
But he cries unto all, "Come taste and see,
"Come try me, and prove me, and thou shalt be
"Convinced I am mighty to save, and so
"The Truth of my proffers thy heart shall know."
Thus the volume of God is open thrown,
And if it were false it could soon be known.
But where in the sea of humanity, wide,
Is one to be found who thoroughly tried,
And met its conditions all pure and good,
And proved it not truly the Book of God?
No witness can rise 'neath the heaven's blue
And aver that he knows the Book's untrue.
While all who have tested its remedy,
By their faith in the Truth have been made free.
With uplifted hands, and face aglow,
They shout, Hallelujah! *I'm saved! I know!*
What a fund of knowledge their faith hath wrought,.
While the skeptic's faith hath gathered naught.
'And why not believe in the truth so high?
Because they believe, yes "believe a lie."

    And now let us see what that faith hath done,
The believing that believes God's Son.
Sure as the heart that confides in the Lord,
Believes not the devil a single word,

So sure he believing not Christ Divine,
In the devil is trusting all the time.
Pure Eve, the mother of all the living,
Never doubted the warnings God had given,
'Till believing the words of hell's devise;
So all doubting truth is intrusting lies.
All the just do live by faith, very true.
So the wicked by faith their course pursue.
Not a lost man walks where the tidings shine
But by faith in error he lives in sin.
True grace and glory, and every blessing
God offers to all, but the foolish listen
To the blinding song of earthly mammon,
And like Eve discredit high Heav'ns larum.
Trust hell to-day, presume for the morrow,
And "pierce themselves through with many a sorrow."
Through faith in satan neglect salvation,
And drown their souls in hopeless perdition.
The young are warned by their aged sires,
To flee from the serpent of vain desires.
The Bible bids high for their youthful days,
And virtue would lead them in pleasure's ways.
Give riches and honor and sweet content,
And crown them in Heaven, with their consent.
They behold that righteousness tends to life,
And sinful indulgence to mis'ries rife.

But they listen to 'witching songs of fame,
Or the pleasures of sin enchant their-brain.
And pride chimes in with her flattering tongue.
Reason fails, he believes, is swept along
"In the course of this world," and hopeless dies;
Lost forever through faith in satan's lies.
When's the time to be saved? Shall wisdom say?
Loud she cries from Heaven, "to-day!" "to-day!!"
Lo! now is salvation's accepted time!
To-day while thy reason and breath are thine!
Do ye hear it, ye earless who persevere
In sin? Why then to satan still give ear?
Ah! such is the leaning of man depraved!
Discrediting truth by evidence paved,
Yea! truth which his reason and highest good
All vindicate loudly; and true man-hood
Would choose for her building, her only ground.
But rashly believing the soothing sound
Of demons all harping, "not now," "not now!!"
There is time enough yet. why need you bow?"
This folly believes, and without one proof,
And from heavenly counsel stands aloof.
So the wicked by faith hold on their way,
With the torments of hell their faith to pay.
Yea whatever the hook or crook may be,
That keeps him unwilling to bow the knee,

'Tis faith in the devil who breathed the lie,
Just as truly as saints on God rely,
When they venture their souls upon His will,
And follow their Lord in self denial.
Then Mr. Skeptic just please remember,
You live in sin by faith in your father,
As much as the saint, you call weak minded
Believes in the truth of God, well found.
If counted weakness of mind to rely
On the Infinite God, who cannot lie,
Have ye an occasion your minds to praise,
Trusting in satan the father of lies?
True you know not your father as do we,
Since from his dark thralldom our souls are free.
And as to our Father, Creator of all,
Ye never have known Him, else would ye fall
At the feet of His Son, and life implore,
And, saved out of darkness, His name adore.
  But men slight God in the pride of their hearts,
Oft wishing His favor when life departs.
Some vaunt in health their infidelity
But wake to sober thoughts and honesty
To call on God—alas! sometimes too late—
When approaching doom reveals their awful state.
As did the blind fool-hearted Tuttle
Who was the devil's active shuttle

To weave, through life, a web of lies,
He wished in bitter tears he'd ne'er devised.
Who wrote and formed in maddened strife,
Against the holy saving Book of life.
Then bowed at last when old and gray,
And tried in bitterness of soul to pray
At the public altar in the tented camp,
All doctrines of the devil he did fain recant.
But deeply blinded in the way of self-damnation
His half 'waked soul grasped not expiation.
   And so failed the faith of the diest Paine,
When on his death-bed imploring the name,
Of God for help, and the Lord Jesus Christ.
So fails the faith of all sinners at last.
In this, or in the awful world unseen,
They'll awake in woe, from their life's dark dream.

# FAITH'S APPEAL TO HER FRIENDS

Why should I yet be "wounded in the house of my friends."—Zech. 13: 6.

"How long will this people provoke me? and how long will it be ere they believe me."—Num 14: 11.

"Do ye now believe?"—John 16: 16.

"If ye will not believe, surely ye shall not be established"—Isa. 7: 9.

Therefore "Believe in the Lord your God, so shall ye be established; believe His prophets so shall ye prosper."—2 Chron. 20: 20.

"While ye have the light believe in the light." — Jno. 12: 36

"He that believeth not shall be damned "—Mark 16: 16.

"He that believeth on me hath everlasting life."--Jno. 6:47.

"Believest thou this?"—Jno. 11: 27.

"Unto you that believeth He is precious."--1 Peter 2; 7.

Therefore "Be not faithless but believing."--Jno. 20: 27.

# FAITH'S APPEAL TO HER FRIENDS,

HEAR, O friends! my plaintive and chiding song!
Why hang on the borders of doubt so long?
O will ye grasp my hand, and plight your love
To my Author, and thine, who stands above
All just occasion for the doubts and fears
Which ye so often thrust like cruel spears
Into His bleeding heart.   For ye should know,
When piercing me, ye wound my Author too!
Yea more, drive the dagger in your own breast,
And disquiet your souls from peace and rest.
   Hath our Lord exacted too much of thee,
In that faith, so simple, that sets thee free?
Does not satan, meanly disguised,
Hold all his children to credit his lies?
And the crafty old world of sin and lust,
Demands of his children implicit trust
In all his ten thousand arts to deceive.
His humbugging show-bills many believe,
Though badly bitten every time they bite,

The next vaunted bauble is surely all right.
  No fool on earth is so credulous crazed
As the man whose faith is so wildly raised,
That it climbs over wonderful facts that rise,
Like Heaven-lit mountains, above the skies,
Rebuking the madness of sinful man
Who, trusting in fables rejects God's plan.
To reconcile all the stupendous effects,
That faith in the Gospel always begets,
With the skeptic's cry, "Its only fable,"
Taxes credulity more than double
Enough to surmount all the hills that look
So dark 'twixt their reason and Heaven's book.
Hills that are miraged upon their eyes,
By the magic of hell in deep disguise.
So the infidel's faith and sham pretense,
Strains credulity and racks common sense.
  But why should a friend of truth be slow
To venture on the Rock, so tried and true?
Yea, venture his all, and forever more,
Upon the foundation he knows is sure.
Why "devils themselves believe and tremble."
Should men in folly their souls yet gamble,
Yea, barter to hell 'neath a doubt and fear
To brook the dragon, or his subject's sneer?
O Why to the father of lies give ear,

When he'd shoot misgivings within thy breast,
That rise from the feelings he hath depressed?
Have ye not learned that no inward frame
Is the ground of faith, but, ever the same,
The truths of Heaven are beneath thy soul?
And He that hath ransomed will keep thee whole.
Then seek not emotions, nor dig the ground
Of thy feelings, to see if thy faith is sound.
If emotions sweet in thy bosom rise,
Bless the heav'nly odors, but yet be wise,
And mount not upon their ethereal wings,
But stand upon Truth, where faith ever sings.
　　Finally, solemnly, friends of the Truth!
If sound in the faith, let thy works show forth.
Thy soul in sin, with thy hope shall perish,
If a selfish aim thy heart would cherish.
Abhor all evil, walk in love, and crown
The Triune God in thy bosom alone.
If "the work of faith, with power" and love,
And much heavenly fruit, thy life approve,
Then low in the dust of self-denial,
And meek endurance in every trial,
Faith shall bless thy life to the good of all,
Where the light of thy soul like sun-beams fall,
On the hearts that sigh 'neath the shades of death;
And deserts shall blossom by thy touch of faith.

All the world shall yield to thy reign of grace,
And darkness sh ll flee from before thy face.
While angels of glory shall bless thy path
And all Heaven shall crown thy fight of faith.

                              Amen!

# MEMORIALS.

## CELIA.

AND is she gone? dear Celia gone?
    Such news would tax credulity
Did not the Spirit's previous tone,
    Toll in our bosom mournfully.
The thought, "she's left this mortal clime,
    And we shall see her face no more,
Until we pass the bounds of time,
    And meet upon Celestial shore."


'Twas in our heart to tune our lyre,
    To sing thy cheerful wedding day;
But debts are made by fond desire,
    More than our fleeting time can pay:
So now we sing our mournful lay,
    Another epoch followed soon.
To thy poor soul a brighter day
    Than that, when blest beside thy groom.

The Author of these feeling hearts,
  Chides not affection's flowing tears;
But with them soothing balm imparts.
  And in His arms of love He bears
Poor nature's heavy burden up:
  So when bereavements press our mind
Grace drops such sweetness in the cup,
  That even then we comfort find.


But is she gone, whose heart e'er burned
  With such devoted fervent zeal?
To bless mankind her spirit burned
  Wished every heart God's love might seal.
Who thought no sacrifice on earth too dear,
  No painful toil and care too great
That all this world the truth might hear,
  And gain redemption's blissful state.


O sister, while thy eyes beheld
  What e'er thy willing hands could do,
No needed rest thy footsteps held,
  No moderation couldst thou know.
Regarding not thy slender frame—
  To pious toil so passionate--
Till thy enfeebled limbs refrained
  To execute thy heart's mandate.

But hath God quenched that ardent thirst
  To labor in the Lord's employ?
Her active soul in Paradise
  With rest alone would seem to cloy.
Nay, formed to constant action here,
  Which to our Father honor brings,
The soul will find sweet labor there,
  And swifter still unfold her wings.


So we conclude our sister's heart,
  Where glowed such wondrous zeal and love,
Is not compelled with them to part,
  Since gone from earth to realms above;
But Jesus saw her faithfulness,
  And, needing on His higher plain,
One tried and true in holiness,
  Made choice to call dear Celia's name.


And He who placed to her reward,
  Much labor freely given Him,
Saw fit, in kindness to award
  Her soul with patient months of pain.
Tho' oft the prayer of faith was poured
  Around her wasted stricken form,
Relief was temp'ral; for the Lord
  Would have her in His better home.

Now gone from us, but she's not dead,
　Despoiled, 'tis true, her house of clay;
But when that sacred spot you tread,
　Methinks you'll hear an angel say,
"She is not here, to her was giv'n
　A life that soars above the tomb."
The angels bore her safe to heaven,
　Free from mortal pain and gloom.

When sickness had already cast
　Its waning paleness on thy cheek.
God folded thee within the breast
　Of love, connubial, warm and deep.
Thank Heav'n for this provision, kind,
　To bless, support and comfort thee.
On whose strong arm thy life declined,
　Till from thy suffering body free.

God bless you, brother, now bereft
　Of her so dear to you. and all.
To cheer thy heart this boon is left,
　'Twas thine to give, at Heaven's call,
A sacrifice so paramount.
　Beloved on earth. and welcomed home,.
To glory's bright elysian mount.
　By all the angels round the throne.

O God console that heart to-day
  That weeps far in the floral west.
Where love's fine tendrils torn away
  Are bleeding mournful in the breast.
A sister kind, her sister weeps.
  Bless her, O Lord, and all the friends.
While Celia walks the golden streets,
  Where all our bitter weeping ends.

Dear Celia's gone!  How sad the news
  Dear saints! this mourning Trumpet brings.
The hands that dropped refreshing dews
  Upon its flying angel wings,
And toiled so hard to set the lines
  That burned upon your hearts with love,
Inspired your souls a thousand times,
  Has gone to blissful toils above.

Yea sad indeed to us it seems!
  Yet would it not be selfishness.
Did we not bless her boundless gains,
  Since she has lived the world to bless?
Ah! we will always cherish here
  Her sacred name in memory,
And ever keep our title clear
  To meet her in the heavenly.

And gracious God! O bless we pray!
　Dear Rhoda's kind and weeping heart
Who toiled with her in harmony:
　How sad that these dear ones must part!
'Twas meet, dear child, that you should be
　With Celia to her peaceful end,
To bless her with thy sympathy,
　And every comfort to extend.

These four years labor, hand in hand,
　Knit thy two hearts forever one.
God give thee grace yet firm to stand,
　Until thy labor too is done;
Then—O how sweet to contemplate
　That morning when the trump shall sound,
When you shall in immortal state,
　Embrace, and be together crowned!

These thoughts, suggested by her life,
　We give to workers in her stead,
Be diligent, lest labors rife
　Accumulating, grieve the dead.
But let us also profit by
　The dear one's over-reaching toil;
These holy temples, born to die,
　O crush not premature with moil.

Let all this office sacred be
  To Him who called our loved on high.
Each spot recalls her memory,
  Each object here that greets the eye,
By Celia's hands is sanctified,
  Who handled them in Jesus' name:
And now with holy angels glorified,
  Loves yet the truth these type proclaim.


Ah! now invert the column rules,
  And dress the TRUMPET sad with crape,
That all who read, may know it feels,
  And weeps the loss of friend so great.
Her artful fingers shall no more
  Set up its many vocal peers,
Nor shall her anxious heart yet pour
  Upon its sheets her moist'ning tears.


Her gentle voice so fine and sweet,
  The Trumpet organ's highest key,
Is singing now at Jesus' feet,
  With Heaven's joyful minstrelsy.
O could we near the pearly gate,
  And listen to her ransomed song,
Our souls would more felicitate,
  The bliss of that immortal one.

# Lily and Willie.

O LET them go to the Savior's arms.
  And let thy bosom confide
In Him who calleth thy little ones,
  Close to His sheltering side.
He never inflicts a willing pain
  Within a sorrowing breast;
But to our highest eternal gain
  His rod in wisdom is blest.


O let them go!  When the angels came
  To bear sweet Lily above,
They saw dear Willie, and bore his name
  Up to the mansions above.
Then Heaven was pleased and wished him there
  Lest time his innocence sting,
And lest the terrene his beauty mar,
  Sent back the angels for him.

O let them go! for the earth is dark,
  And dangers thickly impend
Where pleasures charm may the serpent lurk,
  'Tis well life's evils are stemmed;
For sin doth spread like a mighty flood
  O'er all our slumbering race.
Thank God! they're gone to a safe abode
  A sweet and Heavenly place.


O let them go! for pity hath seen
  Some cruel tempest ahead,
Some blast of woe, or bitter-most stream,
  To which their journey had led.
God took them in compassion from time
  As lambs unspotted, ungrimed.
O couldst thou know His gracious design
  Thy heart were fully resigned.


Yes, let them go to the better land!
  No grief can follow them there.
We know, O Jesus! Thy loving hand
  Took them to Heavenly care.
Their voice is hushed, and their gentle tread,
  No more their presence we see:
Yet weep we not over them as dead,
  Who live more happy than we.

Ah! let them go! tho' we miss them here,
  Dear Father, bestow Thy grace!
Our eyes, though dimmed by affection's tear
  Would see Thy comforting face;
In all Thy providence love confess,
  And seek to honor Thee more,
That we may follow, and meet in bliss,
  Our loved ones passing before.


O let them go from the house of clay!
  Sweet-uncaged spirits, go home!
Nor let thy thought yet in anguish stay
  Around their mouldering tomb.
Lift up thy faith from affliction's vail,
  And by her vision behold
Thy darling ones over death prevail,
  In bright ethereal fold.


O let them go: in this mortal clime
  We cannot ever remain :
Life lingers not in the bonds of time,
  But seeks eternity's plain.
And death is but a shadow between
  All pilgrims holy and pure,
And their sweet hope's enrapturous scene
  Beyond time's beautiful shore.

# Clara Belle.

DEAR Clara Belle,
   Thou tiny bud
T'is well with thee,
   At home with God.
An infant sweet,
   Has left us lone,
A cherub bright
   Shines at the throne.

O were the vail
   Withdrawn that we
Our little Belle
   On high could see,
The beauty of
   The robe she wears,
Would be enough
   To dry our tears.

So while we miss
   The darling ray
That shone with us
   So brief a day.
We bow to Him
   Who gave the boon,
And took again,
   Alas! so soon.

This earth is dark!
　　Our days are few!
We must embark
　　And follow too,
Across the tide
　　That lies between
This mortal stride,
　　And future scene.

While we yet have
　　A little space,
On earth to live,
　　O save by grace!
That we at last,
　　May come and dwell,
In endless rest,
　　With Clara Belle.

## Sister Ida Spacky.

S O death, as named and feared by man,
　　Is to the saints a hallowed rest;
What joy and peace attend the scene!
　　A soul by angel arms embraced!

How beautiful in Jesus' sight,
The sleep of all the holy ones!
　　We hear a voice from Heaven "write,
How bless'd the death of Zion's sons."

The spirit goes to God at once,
  The conscious, and the real man;
The grave will yield its treasure up;
  And glory crown the blessed plan.


The sting of death is only sin,
  But full salvation sweeps it all;
O! praise the Lord for victory,
  That leaves the grave no dread appall!


Death's kingdom is abolished quite,
  His sting removed in Jesus' blood.
We wake and sleep in Heaven's light,
  And live together with the Lord.


The promise and the love of God,
  A sweet and full assurance give,
That we shall reign in conscious good,
  While God the Son, and Father live.

# Father Beebe.

AH! see upon that tranquil brow,
　The glow of Heaven's peace!
A pledge that Father's Spirit now
　Has found a sweet release.

How beautiful in Jesus' sight,
　The sleep of holy saints!
Yea, saith the voice from Heaven, "write,
　Blessed be their rest from hence!"

The house that long was quickened by
　Dear father's ransomed soul,
Dissolved and left his spirit fly
　To its immortal goal.

His bended form we'll see no more,
　Nor trembling voice will hear,
But treasured in our mem'ry's store,
　We hold his virtues dear.

His walk was gentle, free from strife,
　His pilgrim robes like snow,
The fragrance of his holy life,
　Still lingers here below.

# Arthur L. Morgan.

A GENTLE Hand, unseen by us,
  Has plucked our sweetest bud.
By this alone our grief is blessed,
  It was the hand of God.

In all our hearts He planted deep,
  This precious little one.
As forth He takes His own we weep,
  But say, Thy will be done.

No care was lavished here in vain,
  Upon this plant of love.
Though soon removed, he'll bloom again,
  In sweeter form above.

O gentle one! we miss thee here!
  Sweet form we love so well!
But in our Father's better care,
  We know the child is well.

Would not our grief forever flow
  Upon his silent tomb,
Did not our hearts this comfort know,
  We'll meet in glory soon.

O Jesus! Thou hast died for us,
　And for our darling too.
We'll trust Thee in each providence,
　Thy love is ever true.

## Dr. P. J. Smith.

THE subject of these lines practiced medicine fifty years
Was saved in his last years   His organ of time was so accurate
that at any time, by day or by night, he could tell the time of
day, usually to the minute.   So we were informed by his friends.

JESUS took the pilgrim home,
　His weary life and sufferings o'er;
"And now my children, will you come?
　And meet me on the golden shore.

Master of the passing time,
　Yet heeding not it s golden hours,
Till but few, alas!   were mine,
　And wasted quite my noble powers.

Knowing well the time of day,
　But weighing not it's value great;
Many years have run away,
　In my lost, and erring state.

Like the miller flitting round,
   The dazzling lamp, exposed to flame,
Humans tread on danger's ground;
   Much blinded by earth's gilded fame.

Wisdom sees what others loose,
   And profits by their folly past,
Will you then salvation choose?
   That no regret may sting at last.

## Sister Sarah V, May,

SHE died a saint, well satisfied
   That grace she longed to know,
And precious blood she wished applied,
   Had washed her white as snow.

'Tis well she cherished, warm and true,
   A love for truth Divine.
And always wished that bliss to know,
   Which holy hearts enshrine.

The hand of God can ne'er withdraw
   And leave an honest soul,
Who holds the Book of God in awe,
   And longs to be made whole.

"I wanted much to be a saint,
  But knew not how to grasp;
But now, thank God! my heart is white.
  And I'm a saint at last.


"Farewell my friends, now let me bathe
  My lips and cool my brow.
For O! I see the angels wave
  A welcome for me now.


"Farewell now let me sweetly rest,"
  And so she closed her eyes,
And placed her hands upon her breast,
  And, as the wavelet dies,


Upon the ocean's laving shore,
  She sank to sweet repose.
Her soul redeemed forever more,
  To worlds of beauty rose.


As on her raptured spirit burst
  The glories of that place,
A smile showed how her soul was blest,
  Which lingered on her face.

# A Young Man.

SON and brother, hast thou left us ?
    Must we bid thee long farewell ?
Nature weeps, but Jesus whispers,
    Let him come with me to dwell.

Must thy goodly form unfolding,
    Into manhood's noble prime,
Early drop to silent mold'ring,
    'Neath the busy tread o.' time?

But thy disembodied Spirit,
    Sin and sorrow sweeping by,
Through the dear Redeemer's merit,
    Rose to Paradise on high.

From the din of earthly battle,
    Ere thy hopeful noon had come,
Jesus called thee to a better,
    To His safe Eternal home.

Ere the silent chord was broken,
    And the scene of life was closed,
Jesus kindly whispered pardon
    To thy heart, on Him reposed.

Just redeemed from sin's dominion,
    Then the summons came for him.
And his happy ransomed spirit
    Shall in endless glory sing.

O the wondrous! wondrous story!
  Brother's safe at home with God!
Ransomed from this earth to glory
  Washed in Jesus' precious blood.

## Nancy Howe.

OUR mother has gone to the land of rest,
    That beautiful home where the angels dwell,
Now safe in the bosom of Jesus blest.
    Though lonely, dear Lord! we bow to thy will.

Our hearts are clinging, dear mother to thee,
    Thou livest here yet, in each bosom of love.
Our mem'ry shall cherish thy gentle form,
    Till we meet thee, dear mother, homed above.

Thy virtues still shine in our saddened home;
    Endearing each object thy hands have wrought.
And leaving to us the legacy, pure,
    Thy holy and innocent life has bought.

O mother!  dear mother!  we miss thee so,
    Unthinking, we listen for thee to come.
But Jesus will comfort, and grace bestow;
    And lead us to join thee in Heaven's bright home.

# HYMNS.

## My Soul is Satisfied.

ALL this earth, its wealth and honor,
  Cannot sate the human breast,
But when filled with God our Father,
  Every want is fully blest.

All my soul can wish forever,
  I do find in Christ replete.
Every blessing and the Giver
  In my peaceful bosom meet.

Is thy life bereft of comfort?
  And thy heart a cheerless spot?
Say not Christ is in thy desert;
  For we can believe it not.

Can a bird drink up the ocean,
  Thirsting still from shore to shore?
Or the God of all creation
  Leave thy heart yet craving more?

Would my soul could more encompass
  Heaven's glory willed to me.
O the love of God, so precious!
  'Tis a deep and shoreless sea.

# Christ the Friend We Need.

OFT my heart has bled with sorrow,
    Not a friend my grief to share.
But I yielded Christ to follow,
    And He took my load of care.

Long I sighed for peace and pleasure,
    Felt a painful void within.
Life was gloomy, death a terror,
    Till my soul was saved from sin.

All this world is dark and dreary,
    And the soul, designed for light,
Must be sad and lost forever,
    While it gropes in sinful night.

Oh my soul in sin was wretched,
    Dark the shadows round me fell:
Jesus blessed and calmed my spirit,
    Saved me from the fears of hell.

Sin made all my life so bitter,
    Jesus makes it sweet and pure
Oh!   I'm free from ev'ry fetter,
    Blest with peace forever more,

# The Temple of God.

NOT in the temples made by hands,
　　Tho' so beautiful by art,
But God in mercy condescends
　　To dwell within my heart.

How wonderful that Jesus would
　　Enter this abode of sin!
And wash me in His precious blood,
　　And now abide within.

No more I think of God afar;
　　For thy glories inward beam.
O shine thou blessed Morning Star,
　　And keep thy temple clean.

Far greater is the Mighty One,
　　Dwelling in me all the time,
Than all the world and hell can sum,
　　And 'gainst my soul combine.

O Lord! enshrined within my breast,
　　Fountain of eternal peace,
My soul can now forever rest,
　　Secure in thine embrace.

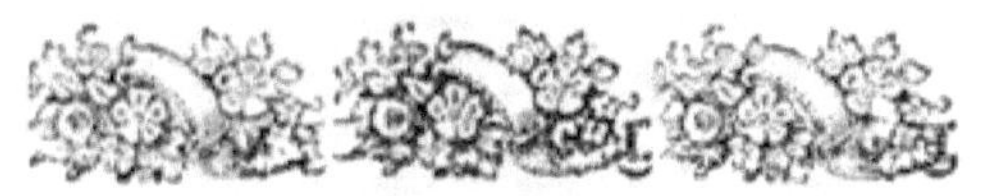

# CONTENTS.

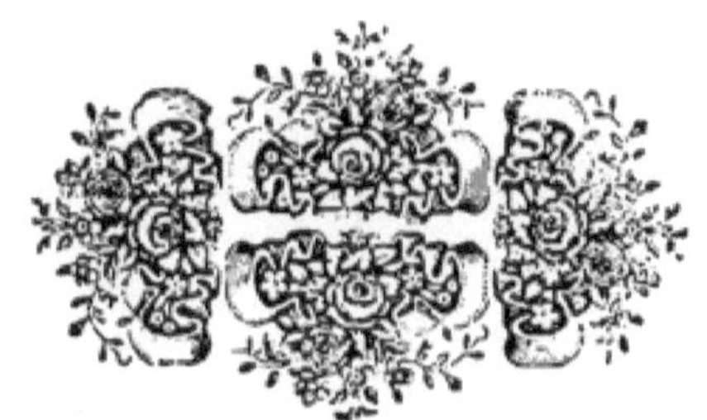